Two Similar Looking Men with Umbilical Hernias

WRITTEN BY

Zena Barrie

WITH ILLUSTRATIONS BY

Claire Robinson

Breakthrough Book Collective

Published in Great Britain in 2025 by Breakthrough Books.

www.breakthroughbookcollective.com

Paperback ISBN: 978-1-0684124-5-5

Ebook ISBN: 978-1-0684124-6-2

Cover design and interior typesetting by Ivy Ngeow.

Front and back cover image: Claire Robinson, 2025

Dearest Meredith,

One day I will hopefully write a beautiful and widely celebrated work of literary fiction with a strong feminist angle that will really change the way people view the world; and I will dedicate it to you, and you will be proud of me.

But just in case that doesn't happen....

For Meredith XXX

(I hope you enjoy all these stories about hernias, haemorrhoids, periods and bull semen)

About the Author and Illustrator

Zena Barrie is quite nice.
She can sometimes be self-important, two-faced and slovenly.
Special skills: bendy arms & popping ears
Star sign: Scorpio

Claire Robinson is quite pompous but bubbly. She likes making cakes in other people's houses and leaving all the washing up.
Special skills: can wear any bonkers old shit and still look stylish, even at her age.
Star sign: Libra

Together they are bosom friends, like Anne and Diana[1]. Although Diana was a bit basic so not exactly like Anne and Diana. These completely true stories (if you can call them that) are ... let's say fiction, and if they bear any resemblance to people living or dead let's say that's a complete coincidence. Although they[2] do say there's nothing new under the sun...

---

1. Anne of Green Gables and Diana Barry from *Anne of Green Gables* by Lucy Maud Montgomery.
2. In this case 'they' are Ecclesiastes 1.9 in the Old Testament, written by someone called Solomon who was probably quite wise but also very religious. Swings and roundabouts...

Author's Note

This book is for over 18's because the publisher said it had to be, amongst some of the many other things she said about it.

Contents

THE ORIGINAL UMBILICAL HERNIA MAN

Someone once told me that going for a sauna is as good for your heart as going for a run. I didn't need telling twice, I now go to the sauna often and it can be pretty chatty in there. If you are looking for a quiet but very hot place to contemplate life, this would not be the sauna you are looking for. There are others that might have less going on in them.

Do your own research.

One morning, around 6.45am, I was already in there, sweating away and chatting to a man with a very obvious umbilical hernia.[1]

I know about umbilical hernias because I watch an unreasonable amount of medical dramas, and also, I had an ex that had an umbilical hernia. He had to have surgery, and afterwards he no longer had a belly button; which made him look as inhuman as he turned out to be.

---

1. An abnormal bulge that can be visible where the belly button should be. It occurs when things that should be inside the body start pushing their way out for some inexplicable reason. It's nothing good. That's all you need to know

It was very early, I didn't quite have my head screwed on yet for the day (yes, this is a terrible excuse for what is about to come) ... and so I said to the man:

"Oh, you have an umbilical hernia"

"Yes," he said, "it's fine."

Clearly trying to shut this line of enquiry down fast.

But I knew it might not be OK, because I'd seen an episode of *Grey's Anatomy* where every time a man coughed, all of his internal organs popped out of his chest wall and into an external hernia sack. And so, I ploughed on, and described to the man what I had seen on *Grey's Anatomy* in great detail. I went on to say that with all this in mind, perhaps surgery would be a good idea?

The Umbilical Hernia Man got up and left the sauna.

It quickly dawned on me just how inappropriate I had been. He didn't need me to point out his hernia. It was HIS hernia. He knew all about it. And I am not a doctor ... although I reckon I could easily pass myself off as a pretty effective GP.

"What's wrong? You're feeling ill? Live in the city? Have some anti-depressants and an inhaler... Got a temperature? I'm sure you've got a few leftover antibiotics in a drawer somewhere. Next!"

Anyway, I felt terrible about Umbilical Hernia Man and my behaviour towards him. I would not appreciate a complete stranger surveying my body without invitation and telling me I needed urgent surgery.

And so...

I started going back to the sauna on the same day, at the same time, hoping I would see him again and get the chance to apologise. For months I kept waking at 2am thinking about Umbilical Hernia Man.

Then one morning, after many fruitless and sweaty mornings, there he was.

Sat in the sauna on the bottom step, his umbilical hernia more protrusive than ever.

I let myself in and sat across from him, preparing myself for the apology that I had now been thinking of for months.

As I sat on the hot wooden bench trying to construct an opening sentence in my head, the sauna door opened and in walked another man ... with an umbilical hernia.

I looked back and forth at each man. I looked back and forth at each umbilical hernia.

I could not tell which man was the original umbilical hernia man.

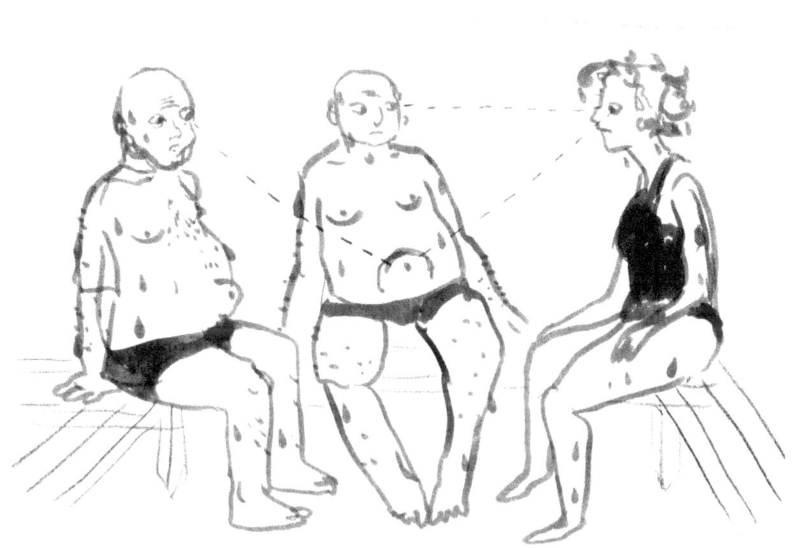

The Last Egg

I t's been 63 days
        And no period.
        Is that it now?
Can I finally go out and buy white trousers and roller skates?

Is there one last egg in there, pottering around like Moses in the dark with no one to speak to? Maybe sweeping up a little and turning off the lights?

Why did he never get picked to slide down the fallopian tube? It must have been quite good fun. I bet the other eggs enjoyed that. Did he always draw the short straw?

He can't have been on his own for too long, he must really miss all the other eggs. The eggs that had been hanging around for so long they got cynical. If they met some sperm they'd pepper spray it before it ever got near. They'd handcuff it to a radiator and question it for hours.

"What the fuck are you doing in here? Who gave you a key? This is OUR place. What do you expect from us? What were you hoping for? Never going to happen buddy, we've got our own thing going on here, we sit around on sofas talking about the glory days, laughing, gifting each other candles, doom scrolling, eating cheese and then having an early night."

Will I eventually fire him out whether he wants to leave or not?

Or will he stay there forever as a sort of janitor, just keeping tabs on things? Will he talk to himself and will the walls echo? Does he feel around the walls looking for an exit like a French mime artist, permanently trapped inside a box? Will he miss the time when the walls got thick and bouncy and he had all the other eggs to play with? Will he be cold in there? I suppose this elderly man is still my child isn't he, of a sort? Just because he can't get out does that mean I shouldn't nurture him? I wonder if he likes me taking warm baths or does that cause some terrible flood where all his bookshelves get soggy?

Jesus...

I'm worrying about some fictional old egg man and planning on ways I can put myself out in order to make his life more comfortable. Why is my brain so quick to be oppressed by a tiny fictional Moses egg?

I will have to squeeze out another period ... somehow. Just one final biblical style period where I can push him out on a giant tidal wave of blood and down the toilet. I don't need an elderly janitor hanging out inside me.

Sorry, tiny elderly egg-man janitor baby, you've got to go, but maybe it will be a wild ride down the sewers, you can surf your way along the pipes on a maxi pad[1] until you reach the ocean. Maybe you'll end up inside a whale if you're really lucky and you can take up residence there. You will have lots more room, you'll have more company, you might get a new lease of life. You might meet loads of cool fish and be there to welcome them when they arrive and tell them not to panic. (Apparently fish panic a LOT when they realise they've been swallowed. It's much better for them to accept what's happened to them and embrace the digestive process.)

It's been 77 days now.

He's all packed up and ready to go.

I've asked him not to leave in the night without saying goodbye.

Sometimes they do that.

I told him that would make me feel bad. If he left without saying goodbye.[2]

All he's got left is just his tea and coffee making facilities[3] and a small stool.[4]

If I ever have to go into a care home, I imagine it would be like this. All your boxes have been carried away and you're not allowed to get them back. You have to go and live in one room with broken furniture in it and horrible mass-produced art. You want to call a friend and say "Fuck it, I've seen some cheap flights to Morocco, shall we go?" but you can't because they're dead and your passport ran out years ago. You could complain to the nurse about the broken ugly furniture but she'll be too busy to care, she'll just think you're a moany old cunt.

---

1. Don't worry, I wouldn't really flush a maxi pad, I'm not a complete cunt.
2. I wouldn't mind that much to be honest, it's just all the washing it creates.
3. Mellow Birds in the morning, Yorkshire Tea in the afternoon.
4. To sit on, I don't mean a small lump of faeces.

It's been 96 days now ... the old man has sent me an ultimatum in my dreams. Push him out now or he will just press his face into the wall and be absorbed.

I'm glad this particular egg didn't become an actual baby; he seems like such a monumental pain in the arse.

Survival

Lost in the wilderness, the wind pounded his face.

Starving and alone, he was desperate.

He just needed something to eat, enough to give him the energy to keep going, to keep walking for just one more day.

He managed to make a small fire, then he carefully tied off his haemorrhoids using some floss.

He fried the haemorrhoids[1] and fashioned them into a small pie. It ended up looking a bit like a mince pie. 'Happy Christmas,' he said to himself as he took the first bite.

He ate it and it sustained him for a day.[2]

The next day, after travelling many more miles, he set up camp for the night. He reached into his trousers, hoping to harvest more haemorrhoids but alas, they don't grow very fast.

He cut off a finger instead and fried that, sucking greedily on the bone and then popping it into his rucksack to make a bone broth soup with it the next chance he got. He'd seen Nigella do something sort of similar, though admittedly not with her own fingers.

Perhaps, he thought to himself, perhaps there will be more haemorrhoids tomorrow...

But they were quite slow growing. Certainly, too slow growing for him to be able to rely on them as a permanent solution to his malnutrition.

His morale left him when he didn't have enough fingers left to start a fire because he'd eaten them all.

He did make it home, which is remarkable. 'How?' you're asking. 'I don't know,' is my reply, don't shoot the messenger. Do your own research.

After he had recovered a little, he started to think about monetising his bad luck and thought perhaps Channel 4 would like him to front a programme about survival. But they didn't, they found him

---

1.   Little bum grapes that hang out around your arsehole made of congealed crusty blood.

2.   Like that fish you sometimes hear about, you know, should you give a man a fish or a fishing rod? They never worry whether he's fond of fish or fishing. They don't offer him a cow or a machine gun. Always a bloody fish.

distasteful. He could tell after he had a meeting with them and one of them spat out "Are you fucking kidding?" whilst the other sniggered.

Sometime later he got a job in an office and became the office bore. People would ask who was going for lunch, or what had people brought in for their lunch, and he would never fail to wang on about how he didn't have to go to PRET a Manger because he could get a free nutritious meal by just reaching into his own pants. (His haemorrhoids now grew quite prolifically. Again, please don't ask how.)

He developed a philosophy of his own where he argued that humans could and should be completely self-sustaining if they wore clothes made of their own hair and ate their own haemorrhoids. He made up some crap about it being good for the planet and that everyone should do it or die if they are unable to.

He was invited onto *This Morning* and Gino De Campo reluctantly made some of our hero's haemorrhoids into Duck a L'Orange.[3]

He was invited on a podcast to talk about his ideas and was quickly shot down by the interviewer who said that they didn't have any haemorrhoids.

Our hero argued, "Unfortunately, with humans, it's the survival of the fittest."

The podcaster argued back, "So you're saying I should starve? Die? Do you think it's better for a person to have haemorrhoids than not have them? It doesn't sound very healthy."

The podcaster said that he personally kept a very tidy bum-hole area. He would not welcome the arrival of haemorrhoids. Even if it did mean a steady supply of free protein.

"Well," said our hero, "it's not my fault you can't be self-sustaining, it's tough luck, there will always be runts."

"So, you think I'm a runt? That only people with haemorrhoids should live? That you're some sort of master race?"

---

3. The recipe for this is bum grapes, some duck and an orange, season to taste. There are better things to make though.

"Yes," said our hero unconvincingly and with a hint of defiance. "I am some sort of master race".

Dear Diary,

There's a pandemic[1] going on which means I can't go to the sauna.

It's irritating because I really wanted to see the umbilical hernia men.

I just can't seem to stop thinking about them.

There must be a way of telling them apart.

They're not twins after all. Although they are both bald, with no body hair to speak of, late 50's to early 60's, and they do both have protruding umbilical hernias. I couldn't guess at their political leanings. I have heard it said that an army uniform is a great leveller, but honestly? Put any bald man in a pair of swimming trunks and I wouldn't be able to tell rich man from poor man.

Unless I looked at the label of his trunks and heard him speak.

Or if he had a weak chin and looked particularly inbred.

---

1. I am talking about the coronavirus outbreak of 2020, not to be confused with the Spanish Flu of 1918 as documented on *Downton Abbey* where Lord Grantham heroically doesn't shag his maid because his wife is dying in the next room.

Ice Cream Made from Semen Dream

(as in ejaculate not sailors)

Last night I dreamt that one of the dads from school had set up a new business.

He had decided to make ice cream from his own semen.

I listened to what he had to say about his ice cream and then I said I thought perhaps it would be a difficult business to scale up.

He said I was underestimating what a virile man he is.

I said, even with your virility, I suspect you won't have the same ability to produce ice cream as, for example, the local Vienetta factory.

He looked at me like I had just stabbed him through his heart.

I then asked him if he thought there would be much call for this type of ice cream? For example, would people choose it from a menu of ice creams that included Mivis, Fabs, 99's made out of bog-standard ice cream, Magnums, etc? He angrily asked me what did I know about business start-ups? He said I was forgetting about Heston Blumenthal's famous snail ice cream, that people travel for miles to try it, and perhaps I should be more open to new ideas. He said he was going to speak to some local fancy restaurants and set up a tasting session to see if he could be a valued local supplier.

I said he seemed to have everything worked out.

Despite this being a dream, I will never be able to look at him or speak to him ever again.

My subconscious obviously knows something I don't.

I can't decide how to tell his wife.[1]

---

1. I will probably post her a copy of this book with a Post-it note sticking out of this page and a note on it that says, "This is about your sicko husband."

The Hairdresser

I went to get my hair dyed.

I'm a natural white.

As he scraped my hair with his metal comb I winced and so he said to me, "Beauty is pain, unfortunately."

I nodded back enthusiastically. "Yes," I agreed, "beauty is pain."

But why? Lambs are beautiful, are they in pain?

Look at cows ... so beautiful. Are they in pain?

Do giraffes look at us through their naturally long eyelashes and think we're ugly?

I will make more effort next time I go to the zoo.

I do not want to be silently judged by those long-necked fucking furry dinosaur freaks.

I wonder if giraffes get jealous of leopards for having a much more iconic fur pattern? Probably. And why do they insist on being freak- ishly tall? Someone should tell them, it's a zoo, not bloody Jurassic Park. Get with the programme, lanky necks, everyone else is down here. If they would consider evolving for just ONE SECOND perhaps people would consider having them as pets. Then they could stop being wild and wear Christmas jumpers like all the other animals with some decency. Pet shops would be able to sell a great range of treats for giraffes, including plastic trees for them to feed from. You would just have to stick the fake leaves made from reconstituted meat on the plastic branches for the new, smaller giraffe to feed from. Perhaps we could do some sort of breeding programme with them to give them cute little snubby faces?

Anyway, did I mention I went to get my hair dyed?

VICTORIANS

Today I have woken up and lamented the fact that there are no doctors in my social circle.

Or in fact, anyone at all with any sort of useful job or discernible skill.

Call me though if you ever need an emergency performance artist.

The Victorians would have hated us… Though they'd perhaps be too busy building intricate sewage networks, making iconic fireplace surrounds or designing key infrastructure to notice that we weren't doing much apart from sending the odd tweet, taking photographs of plants and inexplicably counting our steps.

Not all Victorians were master-craftsmen, though. Many of them spent their days master-*bating* over chair legs, and I wonder what they'd make of the chairs we have these days? I can't see them finding my swivel chair attractive.

If Victorian men built a time machine and were able to visit the 21st century they'd soon get to grips with the internet and then they would be phoning in sick to "intricate tile duty at the sewers" whilst they built up their ONLYFANS special channel for people that liked sexy chair legs.

THE INTERNET PART 1
PIGEON RESCUE

Group description

This is a UK group that focuses on the rescue and welfare of wild or feral pigeons in the UK and Ireland only.

Please note – We are not some kind of 'organisation' which 'sends people out' to collect birds. Age limit: must be 18 to join.

Shaun   Hi everyone, my name is Shaun, nice to virtually meet you! This is my friend Pip the Pigeon. I have looked after him for almost a week now. I feed him on mealworm pellets soaked in some water to soften them. I think he may have fallen from his nest. It was a good job I got to him before my 4 cats did! Is there anything else I should be feeding him? Although I have to say, he does seem to be thriving!

Aya Pigeons are vegetarians. Did you not know that? Please feed him good seed and peanuts as a treat. Have you already identified a rehab & rescue centre to prepare him for soft release?

Shaun What is a soft release?

Carol Please put your 'location' on the original 'post' at the top as stated in the group's 'rules'. You can offer him or hand feed him defrosted peas too. He will need to go and join other young woodies in an aviary as he grows up to learn how to be a pigeon and develop flying skills and a wariness of people before being soft released.

Shaun What is a soft release please? And thank you for the advice. His mum, dad and his siblings are in the trees of a neighbour's garden. I was hoping he may go back to them as soon as he is strong enough.

Carol Shaun, his best chance is as I've described, he really needs that aviary time to get prepared for the wild. If you just let him out once he can fly, he's not got much chance of long-term survival, and without getting wild again he is likely to approach humans for food if he gets hungry and that has the potential to not end well for him.
I.E. HE WILL PROBABLY DIE.

Help the Wildlife   Hello, I work at a wildlife rehabilitation centre. Shaun, if you drop me a line, we can arrange for you to drop off your friend Pip. Thanks for helping him.

Shaun   Thanks, I will DM you now.

Janet   Shaun, he is unlikely to survive because of you. He will need an expert to raise him if he is to survive, he has no survival skills. He needs to go to a rehabilitation centre and he needs it NOW. You think you've helped him? You've not.

Carol   Shaun, I see you have a couple of suggestions for where your little guy can go to finish growing up and be safely released. I totally understand how attached you can get to these lovely birds; I've been caring for them for years and each and every one tugs at my heart. You must give him up though, no matter how much it hurts.

Jayne   Wood pigeons don't eat mealworms, he will end up really sick if he isn't given the correct diet. He may grow but he will not thrive. You shouldn't be cuddling him like that either. Pip is a wild animal.

Shaun   I am doing my best. I didn't want my 4 cats to get him. He really isn't doing so bad. What was fluff when I first found him is now coming out as lovely feathers. I am going to take him to Help the Wildlife tomorrow. Thanks all.

Margaret   I had mine nearly 4 weeks she's gone to a rescue centre now. I loved cuddling her; she was such a poppet. I miss her.

Julie   Margaret, you shouldn't have kept a fledgling, (that's the correct name for a baby pigeon) for 4 weeks. She will probably have died since you let her loose. Most likely from starvation. Not a great way to go…

Don   Thank you for noticing him and looking after him you are lovely to have helped him … ignore the lectures.

Julie   He hasn't helped him though. All comments recommending keeping, cuddles etc will be deleted. As a group we do not advocate keeping healthy wild birds as pets, or imprinting them. Telling people facts isn't a 'lecture'. This pigeon, Pip the pigeon, won't be developing properly as he will be malnourished.

Shaun   He doesn't look malnourished.

Julie   Shaun, are you a vet?

Louise   Julie, I don't like your tone. It is possible to be kind, even when BIG mistakes have been made.

Sarah   Telling him to ignore advice and cuddle him isn't going to help. Being fed mealworms for this long at this stage in development is disastrous. He will need the help ASAP. He should be taken to a VET. NOW. He / she might need their stomach pumping!

Shaun   He looks fine. I'm dropping him off at a wildlife centre tomorrow.

Sarah   Tomorrow may be too late unfortunately; the damage has been done. The vet will probably just put Pip to sleep. By the way, is Pip short for Phillip or Philippa?

Aya   He doesn't know how to feed it, I doubt he's correctly sexed it. It takes a trained eye to do this. They don't have huge penises or visible labia (these parts are hidden underneath their feathers). Have you ever seen a pigeon's dick? Either flaccid or erect? I don't think so.

Sarah   He might have rummaged under the feathers to find Pips penis and / or labia?

Mary   I could take him in. I rehab all sorts of wildlife, squabs (the proper name for a baby pigeon) hedgehogs, foxes, frogspawn, badgers etc. Unfortunately, you have been doing the exact opposite of the right thing for this little squab.

Aya   For god's sake, he shouldn't be living with frogs and foxes. The foxes will eat him as soon as they see him, what a mad thing to suggest. You need reporting.

Mary   Also if he was scratched by a cat, he should see a vet and get antibiotics within 24 hours of the incident. It seems you have not bothered to do this though.

Shaun   He was not scratched by my cats, I rescued him from my cats before they touched him.

Mary   Well for future reference since you mentioned having cats... Honestly if any cat has attacked him, he'll be dead soon due to infection from the saliva. Cats saliva is deadly to baby pigeons, squabs or fledglings.

Linda   This young man has a good heart, we need more people like him! However, I understand it's illegal to keep them as pets. Shaun, do you already have a criminal record? If you do, you could end up with a suspended sentence or worse? Perhaps a short stay in prison or borstal depending how old you are?

Mark   I went to borstal in the 60's, was a bit of a tearaway in my younger days. Mostly just mugging people and the odd petrol bomb through a letter box and some bigger robberies and GBH. I wasn't a pigeon botherer though, if he does go down for this, they'll probably put him with the nonces.

Carol   He should not be in this group if he isn't old enough to go to 'adult' prison. The group rules clearly state 'you must be 18 to join this group'.

Shaun   I didn't know it was illegal. I'm dropping it off at the wildlife centre tomorrow.

Mary   Honestly you shouldn't be keeping cats and pigeons together. It's not good for the pigeons or the cats. If your cats have been exposed to pigeon faeces (the proper name for pigeon shit) you should take them to the vets who will probably put them on antibiotics (or put them out of their misery).

Shaun   I do not keep pigeons with my cats. I'm going to leave this group now as I have a plan for Pip. Thanks all.

Nicola   You know he'll probably die, Shaun? STOP FEEDING HIM MEALWORMS. Never mind, you weren't to know. People don't learn about this stuff at school anymore. Teachers are ignorant and lazy. You've joined this group and asked for our help and now you don't want to hear it? Good riddance to BAD RUBBISH. Rest in peace Pip the Pigeon.

You never had a chance with ignorant cunts like this, may you be luckier in the next life.

Mo   You really do need to pass him on to someone better equipped to deal with a fledgling. Keeping him for so long and feeding him all types of meat etc is asking for trouble. Because the reality is, he's not a pet or a natural carnivore and needs to be with his own kind ... though they will probably reject him now because he's tame. You couldn't take a lion out of the circus and just let him loose in Africa and hope for the best. The lion would be looking for the ringmaster or anyone holding a chair and wearing a bolero style jacket. Not hunting wildebeest like he would need to do to survive and to find a mate.

Lotty   Mine like frozen peas, you are doing great. I looked at YouTube for advice on feeding a baby pigeon.

Mo   Was the youtuber a VET? If not, YouTube is not the place to go to for advice. Would a pigeon have access to frozen peas in the wild? You're lucky they haven't choked to death on them.

Sandra   I live in a flat and have 12 lickle pigeons and made them lickle dungarees so they don't poo on my floor.

Mo   Are you kidding? Pigeons should NOT be dressed in human clothes. Unless specified by a VET.

Sandra   So the lickle pigins don't poo on my floor.

Maureen   What are they doing in your flat?

Derek   Pigeons aren't like penguins. They don't mate forever. A pigeon will have several partners over its lifetime. It's extremely unlikely that Pip's parents are waiting for him in a tree next door, the mother is probably pregnant again. She's probably forgotten Pip ever existed, if that is in fact his given name. It's unlikely that pigeons even bother naming their children. If you let Pip go now, he will almost certainly get eaten. Probably by one of your cats, a fox or a magpie.

Mark   FLYING RATS

Julie   Why would you say such a thing? Pip is a woody, a wood pigeon. NOT a flying RAT as you would suggest. Unfortunately, it looks like Pip will be set free without rehabilitation and will almost certainly die.

Maureen   Where do you live, Sandra? I am going to report you to the RSPCA. Pigeons should NOT be wearing dungarees (unless there is a medical reason).

Mark   The RSPCA won't be interested. It's the RSPB that you should contact. BIRDS not ANIMALS.

Julie   Shaun, if you are serious about raising this squab alone then you will need to buy an aviary and you will need to put in the time to help to rehabilitate him. If you are not prepared to put in that time you need to re-think your plans and maybe think again before you try and 'rescue' an animal that doesn't need rescuing. If you do get an aviary, you will need other pigeons in there that he can learn from. Are you going to try and catch the rest of his family from the neighbour's tree? Have you got a big enough net? Or might you try and drug them using a dart gun? You could probably buy one on the dark web.

Sandra   Are you going to teach him to fly, Shaun?

Julie   A human should NOT attempt to teach a bird to fly. The only person that can teach a squab to fly is another PIGEON.

Carol   I had a pigeon that I taught to fly by throwing him in the air.

Julie   Carol, I have reported you to Facebook. This is FAKE NEWS. Shaun, do not attempt to do this. You could break the squab's legs or wings. It is BARBARISM. Do you think you are David Attenborough? Even he would not attempt to teach a bird to fly, he knows his limitations. He watches rare animals die all the time. Would you teach a baby to walk by pushing it in front of a train? YOU probably would!

Louise   Julie, I really don't think Mark Zuckerberg is going to have a strong opinion on this. You might be better off just reporting her to the police? Whilst Pip might look like he is doing well, his development will have been seriously stunted by stroking him and feeding him mealworms. He is probably incapable of being rehabilitated now; on some level he probably thinks he is some sort of human. He needs a forever home. Somewhere with a big aviary where he can live out his years. Maybe with other pigeons that also believe they are human in some way?

Julie Pigeons can live for up to 10 years. Would you put a baby in a cage for its entire life just because it thought it was a pigeon after spending one afternoon with some pigeons? Or would you do the humane thing and try and help the baby get back to its instinctive human behaviour?

Louise I'm just speaking the truth, it's not my fault you're not evolved enough to hear it. I don't know why you'd leave pigeons babysitting a human baby anyway? That's totally illegal.

Julie Pip will probably die anyway.

Louise Shaun, have you considered wringing Pip's neck? It might be the kindest thing.

help

Tattoo

I was so jealous of my ex's new girlfriend that
I had her face tattooed onto mine.
Then he dumped her and sent me an
email saying he missed me and that he was sorry
and what not.

I said I'd meet him in a week. I went and
got my own face tattooed back on.

It's all a bit of a mess at the moment.
Just waiting for the scab to fall off.

SHREDDER

She fell in love with him from the review he wrote about a shredder on Amazon.

She thought it was ironic. At this point in her life, she enjoyed irony. When she met him though, she realised he wasn't being ironic, he really was THAT interested in shredders. He loved everything about them and thought that every home should have one.

The relationship didn't last long, but longer than you'd expect.

Sometimes, he'd go to work and leave her sleeping in his bed. One day, after he'd left for work, she took photos of his orderly collection of WHICH? Magazines and put them on Instagram, mocking him.

He was alerted to the pictures and became very angry. He ended it with her there and then, which was a relief to him. He had never been comfortable leaving her in the house whilst he went to work. She had left his back door open once, it was a MIRACLE he hadn't been robbed. She couldn't be trusted.

Every time she used a shredder after this (which was 73% more often than most people because she always offered to do it), she thought of him with a mixture of fondness and guilt.

A few years later, she found herself looking for her own shredder on Amazon.

The hairs stood up on the back of her neck when she found an expensive model that had been reviewed by her ex. She ordered it and ticked the 'Did you find this review helpful?' box. She wondered if he would get an alert saying she had found his review helpful. She wondered what feelings, if any, this might raise in him. A small semi perhaps? She liked to think she still had that power. Even after so much time had passed.

When it arrived it really did do everything with great ease. Paper, with and without staples, credit cards and CDs. The box was large and it never got jammed. He was right, it really was the 'Rolls Royce of shredders', with an extra-long extension cord and really very much worth the purchase price.

She decided to review the shredder in the hope that he would see her review.

Her review was reported and removed.

She wondered if he had reported her.

She found another shredder on Amazon and reviewed that instead.

Again, it was reported and removed.

She got incredibly angry. 'How dare he think he's the only person allowed to have an opinion about shredders?' she thought to herself.

She spent the rest of her life being a little bit angry about him, a low buzz in the background of her everyday life. Whenever she shredded from then on it was in anger.

Meanwhile he was oblivious to her reviews of shredders because he'd moved on in his life, finding happiness elsewhere. He'd got married, had a family and spent very little time online because he was so busy with work and his children.

If you'd have asked him, he wouldn't be able to remember her surname or anything much about her. He'd had a few girlfriends through the years and she hadn't lasted long or been particularly memorable. The reviews had been removed because they didn't meet

Amazon's decency standards. For example, she'd put things like 'this is the perfect shredder to buy if you're a complete cunt' and things like that. She thought during this point in her life that swearing was funny but of course we all know it's not.[1]

———————————

1. It is.

After the Men
Had Gone

Let's just live everyone said, let's just live. Let's walk home at night without fear.

Let's go for a run with our headphones on and know that no one is following.

Let's approach our front door without brandishing our keys from 50 metres away.

Let's all know that our friends have got home safely without sitting up waiting for that message before going to bed.

Let's park our cars without fear of ridicule.

We collected up all the knives and guns and they were all handed in to a central location.

A team of sporty women who liked sailing took them out to sea and dumped them.[1]

---

1. Yes, I realise I have polluted the sea and armed all the fish. Let's not think about that for now. Let's not imagine them mobilising in the waters against us. We have enough to worry about.

There was a small skills shortage in the dairy farm.

It was decided that we'd stop our addiction to cow's milk.

The cows were released into the hills to live or die.

The same was done with all the zoos, the animals were all set free. It was thought that they would just get on with their lives and mind their own business.

No one wanted to talk about the zoo releases afterwards except to say it was a fucking disaster...

June had the keys to the sperm bank.

She couldn't be trusted though and started having glamorous-looking babies one after the other that looked suspiciously like George Clooney, Brad Pitt, Tom Cruise[2] etc.

Her home was raided and all her seven turkey basters of differing sizes were removed.

She didn't own a single oven dish.

One of the glamorous looking babies got trampled by a stray rhino.

No one wanted to talk about that either.

A lot got swept under the carpet and the entire project was far from perfect.

Men started creeping out from their underground bunkers and they were allowed to reintegrate so long as they didn't keep harping on about it.

---

2. Don't ask me how or why they had a plentiful supply of A-listers sperm.

CHRISTMAS

He said, "Baby, all I want for Christmas is you."

I said, "What the fuck are you on about? I'm not a baby! I hate being infantilised. I thought you knew that? I've told you enough bloody times."

Turns out it was the lyrics from some song or other.
Anyway, I ditched him and then he stalked me for a while.
Then I smashed his windows in and what not.
Merry Christmas!

Fad Diet

I gained a little bit of notoriety in the 80's for a new diet I invented. You just blew your nose and went to the blood bank regularly to donate your blood until eventually you weighed a lot less.

But people started getting a lot of nose bleeds and fainting a lot and I stepped away from the entire project.

It was difficult because I had been the face of it.

A Bad Thing

The year is 2025 and a new pandemic has hit the UK, become airborne and spread quickly and silently. Munchausen Syndrome by Proxy.[1]

Everyone is accusing everyone else of being sick. People are being kidnapped and taken to the hospital for blood tests they may or may not need so the kidnapper can watch the tests being done and then smile furtively at the doctor.

The doctors have caught it too. Which means they're accusing their patients of being sick; everyone is being tested relentlessly and no one knows what is happening anymore.

A team of scientists have developed a test for Munchausen Syndrome by Proxy and are encouraging everyone to get tested. But they then go on to ask if people could send them videos of being tested and also ask for signed pictures of the doctors.

---

1. Munchausen Syndrome by Proxy is a strange airborne disease. When you catch it, you start telling people they have spots and offer to give them a lift to their GP or the nearest Accident and Emergency. You then flirt with any doctors you can find for as long as possible, until they catch it from you and tell you that you have spots, and then the doctor will take you to see a GP and come in to hold your hand. This goes on forever.

Most of the people working at the test centre have caught the disease and are faking the results if they come out negative, and then offering to take the patients to hospital for an invasive series of tests that they can watch whilst flirting with the doctors and stealing cardboard bed pans.

The Prime Minister was called into a COBRA meeting but didn't turn up because he was taking his son to the opticians for glasses he may or may not need. His son may or may not have faked his symptoms and the optician cannot be trusted to say whether the son needs glasses or not. After the opticians, the Prime Minister and his son are going for colonic irrigations because they both feel the other might have candida in their faeces which will need treating.

The person that gives the colonics will be only too keen to confirm their suspicions. They will do this by email after they get back from having their bunions shaved. A new private company is offering this service that includes a video of the procedure complete with doctor voiceover that you can take home and keep forever.

And the optician may or may not lie about the sons need for eye surgery. And then may or may not offer to go the surgery with him. The surgeon may offer some other treatments.

No one knows how to get out of this situation.

CAN YOU HELP?

Are you sure? You look a bit warm?
I can see the veins protruding on your neck.
They shouldn't be so visible.
Shall I book you an appointment?
I'll come with you if you like?
Let me just get changed before we go.

THE WORKSHOP

She came out of the workshop feeling elated.

In the course of one afternoon, she had entirely reinvented herself.

But as the rest of the group said their goodbyes and filtered away, she felt flat again.

It took her about ten minutes to go back to feeling how she did before The Workshop.

In the following days, now and then, she thought about The Workshop and had a surge of energy.

She imagined an immaculate house, and her with her tight bottom and tiny tits popping off to the gym, her being hyper-focussed, hyper-organised and in control of all elements of her life. She was truly going to live, laugh and love in abundance.

Then she got distracted by Pop Master, cat vomit, emails, work and washing and other stuff.

The Workshop had cost £275.

She recommended it to her friends so they'd waste the same amount of money.

She would discuss it with them after they had been and tell them it had changed her life in order for them to feel a bit shit because it hadn't changed theirs. In turn, they would recommend it to their friends and soon everyone was pretending to live, laugh and love in abundance and nobody was and nobody would say so.

Demand for The Workshop grew and some of the women became Workshop facilitators. Soon everyone was a Workshop facilitator. Everyone was either leading a Workshop or attending a Workshop. It soon felt like if you weren't running a Workshop you were a big fat nobody. Soon there was no one to attend The Workshops because everyone was running one. People would pay other people to attend Workshops so they looked like theirs was popular.

It was a crazy time but it did all eventually fizzle out, like these things do.

Today at the Pool…

I was in the pool doing lengths when I saw one of the umbilical hernia men going into the sauna. I decided to get out of the pool and follow him in.

I knew this was tipping over into odd/creepy behaviour, but I also knew that no one would suspect me, because I would have been going into the sauna anyway; and although people can read my face a little, they cannot read my mind.

There were a few people already in there so there was nowhere I could sit where I could get a good view of the umbilical hernia man.

I decided to climb up to the top step and sit directly behind him. I could see his reflection in the glass doors in front of us, and more importantly, I could see the reflection of his hernia.

Was he man one or man two? I was not sure.

I glanced upwards and we caught each other's eye in the reflection. Had he seen me staring at his umbilical hernia?

I smiled slightly but he did not smile back. It was odd to think that the reflection in the glass was the same hunk of flesh that was sat in front of me.

In the glass he was black and white. In front of me he was full colour. His back reminded me of sliced reconstituted meat from the

80's that was pink and that we weren't allowed to have, often bread-crumbed and possibly with a slice of grey egg in the middle. The man in front of me was not breadcrumbed. Though I could see a small patch of psoriasis under his left shoulder.

I could almost expect the reflection to stand up and walk away leaving the man behind, but of course, they were linked. I thought of the times I had tried to outrun my shadow and given myself an asthma attack. You just can't bloody do it; your shadow always effortlessly keeps up with you, smug bastard.

My inner voice whispered, "This is man one, the original umbilical hernia man." My other inner voice, the one that doubts me, whispered back, "But he might be man two." My doubtful inner voice is annoying but I am grateful for it. It's the thing that holds up the wall between me and my most stupid fucking ideas.

I wonder if Donald Trump or Putin has a doubting internal voice.[1] I suspect not. I wonder whether they could learn to tune into it if they tried meditation. It must be there somewhere. Whispering, "Oy, Donald! Put your mushroom dick away, no one wants to see it."

It wouldn't surprise me if Trump or Putin have umbilical hernias to be honest.[2]

---

1. Having thought about it for a bit, I'm pretty sure Donald Trump is one of those people that does not have an inner monologue.
2. Hernias are most common in men; it is associated with ageing and strain on their tummies. I'm quite sure both of them strain their tummies all the time, whilst either eating burgers or warmongering.

DONKEY SANCTUARY

I got a job in the donkey sanctuary.

I wasn't working directly with the donkeys though; I was selling adoption packs.

A woman phoned up and adopted a donkey called Gladys for her sister who was also called Gladys.

She pledged for a full lifetime of looking after Gladys the donkey and receiving regular updates about her.

Gladys died just after the transaction had gone through.

I called the woman back and broke the news that Gladys was dead.

We established that I was talking about the donkey.

She asked if there were any other Donkeys called Gladys she could adopt. There were not.

She asked for a full refund and said she would re-think her sister's gift. She said someone in the shop she worked in had once said she'd known of a monkey called Gladys at either Blackpool or Chester Zoo and she was going to follow that up. If that didn't work out, she could name a star after her for £19.99.

I suspected she didn't actually give a fuck about the donkeys...

THE NIT NURSE

I married a nit nurse. We got married in 1978 and divorced in 1993.

Eventually I couldn't take it anymore.

"How was work?"

"Well, I went through this kid's scalp and it was full of nits."

"What did you do?"

"Sent a letter to the parents."

"Right. What are we having for tea?"

And then after tea she would scrub her hair and then mine, because we were high risk.

And then she would go through my hair with a nit comb.

I contracted nits 327 times during our marriage. Every time she found one in my hair, she would call it 'a little blighter' and I started to flinch inwardly every time I heard the word 'blighter'. I would sit there and pray for her not to say that fucking word. And she always did, and she always laughed after she said it. Which compounded my misery. And every time she'd send a humiliating letter to my parents.

When they gave her a promotion to start looking into outbreaks of scabies in the local area it was the straw that broke the camel's back.

I left and never went back.[1]

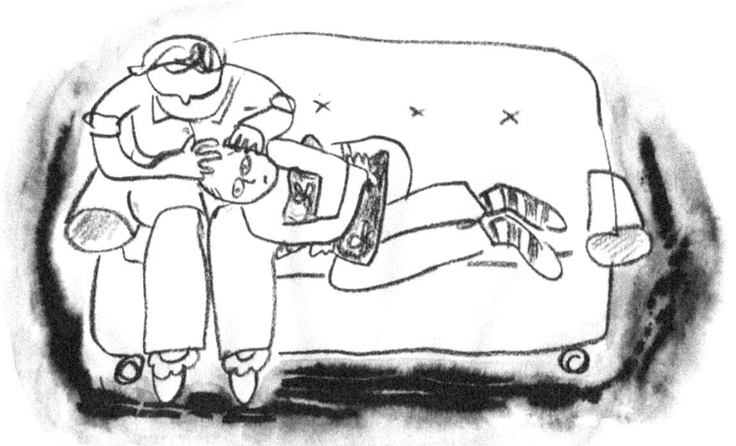

---

1.   Not true, I broke in 1and stole bottles of Vosene and tubes of E45 cream whilst she was at work. I missed the smell, and I missed her. I trawled the internet to find another nit nurse but not a single dating site threw up any search results for nit nurse in the job category. I eventually dated a woman who worked in an STD clinic but she refused to check my pubic hair for lice every day, it just wasn't the same.

Mould in the Utility Room

"There's mould in the utility room," she shrieked.

"What? What? Surely not?" her partner replied.

"Yes, mould ... in the utility room."

"What kind of mould? On some bread?"

"Black mould, the kind that will kill you in your sleep."

"OK, don't panic, close the door, I'm looking on Amazon, there's a spray you can get."

"I'm calling a builder."

"OK, I've ordered six cannisters of mould spray, you spray it on and it kills the mould. You shouldn't stand in the same room as the spray for 30 minutes in case it kills you too."

"I've got a quote from the builder, it'll be eight grand to redo the damp proof course in the utility room. I've booked him in for March."

"OK, I will find us somewhere to live for the next two months whilst that work gets done."

"Whilst we're having that done should we get him to relay the patio?"

"Good idea, I did see some weeds coming up on the patio."

"Weeds on the patio? I'll have a look on Amazon for weedkiller."

"OK, you do that, I'll phone the council."

"Once the utility room damp proof course has been redone, we'll need to redecorate."

"Yes, let's go to Farrow and Ball and get some swatches."

"OK, I need to fill the car up with petrol on the way."

"Yes, and the car needs servicing."

"We can drop in at Halfords, we should get some new mats for the car."

"Yes, and one of those beaded car seats."

"And some eyelashes for the lights on the front of the car."

"No, they're a bit common."

"They're not, I'm sure I read in the *Guardian* that Nigella has them."

"That's OK then."

"If we're doing that, we should get the car resprayed first."

"Oh yes, it did get scratched didn't it, so we must get that repaired as a matter of urgency. Did you call the insurers about that?"

"Yes I did, they're sending round an investigator to check we haven't done it on purpose."

"After they've been, let's go to the Makers Market, they sell recycled cruelty free bags made out of old Coke bottles."

"I'd like to try doing that."

"OK, lets' go to Tesco's and bulk buy some Coke."

"OK, and then we can decant the Coke into some glass jam jars and see if any of the neighbours want it because I don't like Coke but I hate waste."

"Ooh nice idea, that's SO community minded of you."

"I'll look on Amazon and see if they sell empty jam jars, how many do you think we need?"

"At least 100. We could ask the neighbours to give them back when they've finished and then we could use them to make jam."

"Ooh, that's a good idea, I'll buy some fruit bushes."

"Good idea, blueberry and apricot please, strawberry jam is common."

"Do we need some netting to keep the birds off the fruit?"

"Yes, lots of nets, and some broken glass and cement to go on top of the garden wall, we don't want anyone trying to steal the fruit."

"Good idea, and whilst you're on Amazon can you buy a load of wellies, different colours and different sizes?"

"Yes, why?"

"I saw this gorgeous little recycling project where they upcycled old shoes and wellies into plant pots."

"Oh, I love upcycling. There we go, I've ordered 40 pairs, £4 a pop."

"One of us will have to stay at home and wait in for the delivery."

"We should draw straws for it. Have we got any straws?"

"No, I'll have a look on Amazon."

"Good idea. Shall we get those metal ones you can re-use?"

"Ooh yes, they're good for the environment."

"Shall I get the ones with the ivory tips?"

"Ooh, that sounds nice."

"Great, they're more expensive but they give 5% of their profits to the World Wildlife Fund."

"That's worth it, I bloody love animals."

"Do you? We should go on a Safari."

"Good idea, I'll order some guns off Amazon just in case the lions and whatever turn nasty"

"Good idea... and if we did happen to shoot something... do you think we'd be allowed to bring it back and put it's head on a plaque?"

"I'll call the airline and check."

"Good idea."

The Dog

I saw this mangy old dog today.

I wondered where he[1] had been and where he was going to.

He looked like he'd travelled a long way and seen some things in his life, things he could never repeat but were burnt into his soul, and it was written all over his face.

Let's just say, that if his face were a book, it would be the full set of *Encyclopædia Britannica*. (Not the children's editions.)

We briefly locked eyes, he seemed to look right into my soul.

How could a dog I had barely met know me in a way that nobody else ever had? It was so deep, so intimate. There were no secrets left untold.

I had to look away.

He continued on his way down the road. I turned and looked back at him but he did not turn and look back at me.

I was disappointed.

---

1. I say "he" because he had very large, visible, low hanging balls, the likes of which I'd only seen once before and on a man. I forgot to mention this detail though to the artist, so he is presented here without balls. I think you can picture them for yourself. They were almost dragging on the floor. You can draw them on yourself if you like, no one will mind. There are no book police currently.

He had changed my life in a way, and yet I seemed to have made no impression on him at all. Did he look into my soul and see nothing of consequence? I decided there and then to try and read more, lose some weight and clean out my cutlery drawer.

Halley's Comet Steak House

Donald Trump has opened a steakhouse on Halley's Comet. The Cows float from it on a long chain, cooking in the comet's tail.

There is no NHS on Halley's Comet.

There is just a Steak House.

Two toilet cubicles.

A glory-hole (staffed).

A gym for bodybuilding (unstaffed)

and a skip.

Landing spots for rocket ships etc.

A small golf course and a bank (unstaffed).

They've really hiked the prices up, because once you get there it's the only place to eat.

Elon Musk is taking Donald Trump to court because he has paperwork to say he owns Halley's Comet. He says he inherited it from an auntie. He is using the Bayeux Tapestry as evidence. Donald Trump has made an alternative tapestry to prove the comet belongs to him. It's gold and more showy, with more tits on it.

THE ZOO

He shouted at her, "You're not fit to run a zoo, this isn't working![1]"

She looked around at the living room of her small, terraced house and he was right, although she didn't enjoy having it pointed out.

There was excrement everywhere and all the animals looked miserable in this habitat that had been created for them. It was essentially still a functioning sitting room but with some animals in it and a sign saying ZOO.

Most of them were barely moving, there wasn't really anywhere to move to without running into another species. In one corner of the room there was a hedgehog frantically humping a Henry Hoover like his little life depended on it and in the other there were a pair of ferrets[2] going wild over a leftover Pot Noodle.

There was an owl perched on a picture frame that somehow managed to look like all its wisdom had drained from its feet and down the wall.

---

1. I know, I can't stand exclamation marks either... so common.
2. They might have been rats come to think of it.

"Fine, you take over then if you can do it better," she said, petulantly.

He lit a fag and surveyed the room.

Then he said, "I think we need cages or something."

She nodded in agreement; cages would probably be a good idea, although it did go against the founding principle of the zoo, which was to show how people could live alongside animals in harmony without caging them.

His face suddenly lit up. "Let's stuff the dead ones."

She nodded and ran upstairs to find an old pillow.

They could make this work. They had been trying to make this work ever since they read an inspirational Steve Jobs quote...

"We're here to put a dent in the universe. Otherwise, why else even be here?"

They knew that many new start-ups fail or falter in their first 12 months. They were determined not to fail though. As Steve Jobs said:

"You've got to be willing to crash and burn. If you're afraid of failing, you won't get very far."

As they emptied the feather pillow and started stuffing the

contents into a cat which had long since died,[3] they re-affirmed their promise to each other not to let this zoo fail, and there and then they decided to try and find some more exotic animals and to call it the Steve Jobs Zoo.

Later that evening over a few beers, they decided that when they had enough money to pay staff they would make them all wear black polo necks like Steve Jobs, because they'd have the power to make them do that. Perhaps they could get the animals to wear polo necks too and have mini-computers in their cages.

They would open a chain of Steve Jobs zoos all over the country, maybe go global with it?[4] They would maybe contact Apple to see if they wanted to design some special zoo merch? Maybe stuffed animals with phones in them for babies? Or living hamsters with phones in their backs so you can pet them and doom scroll at the same time?

---

3. Long since died of natural causes. No animals were harmed. Repeat: no animals were harmed.
4. Don't worry, it all got shut down before they managed to go global. The animals were rehomed and the couple in question were sentenced to a public stoning.

TALK TO THE ANIMALS

The year is 2033 and we can finally talk to the animals.

Don't ask how, I don't know. *Clearly,* I was not involved with the research.[1]

The first interview was televised live and it was decided we'd start small, with a hamster.

---

1. If you've met me (and let's face it, if you're reading this book you probably have), you would know that I am not the type to get involved with scientific research. Not that I have anything against it per se. I just don't know how to do science. I didn't even want to put my hand through the flame on a Bunsen burner.

It turns out, all that running on wheels is because they feel really bad about themselves, they are absolutely full of self-loathing. All that stuffing their cheeks with food is a symptom of an eating disorder and they can't seem to stop themselves.

The first thing it said was "Can you start this filming again, I wasn't holding my belly in", followed by "Jesus, you would make this breakthrough when I look like shit, fucking typical".

When questioned why the hamster hated its appearance so much it said something like, "How would you feel if you were given an exercise machine from the day you were fucking born? Wouldn't you take the hint and presume you needed to shift some heft?"

They perpetually pass this self-loathing down to their children.

Everyone was very depressed after listening to the interview.

They did have a guinea pig lined up to speak after the hamster but no one wanted to hear it.

The guinea pig was very angry when he found out he wasn't going to get to say his piece. He bit one of his own legs in fury and needed to have stitches.

The vet who had been on hand at the event was running late for an affair with a woman he had met online. She had been the only woman who had responded to the 200+ messages he'd sent to women he didn't know saying, "Hi, how are you today?"

In a rush to use his penis, the vet surveyed the guinea pig's injury and made the decision that the kindest thing to do would be to put him down. Everyone nodded, they wanted to do the kindest thing [2] and also go home and put this whole debacle behind them. (Also they had all been out of their houses for a few hours and they wanted to go home and charge their batteries). [3]

The owner of the guinea pig told the vet he would take the guinea pig home to bury him, but really he wanted to see if he could stuff him or make him into a sporran, he wasn't sure which he fancied trying the most.

He watched a YouTube video on skinning animals. He made a mess of it and after a few days the guinea pig ended up in the outside bin.

The hamster did the PR rounds for a couple of weeks, appearing on the news, *Loose Women* and *Question Time.* But he soon became a figure of fun and swiftly retired into obscurity.

When he died, he was sold to Ripley's Believe It or Not and was put in a cabinet across from a fish that had a human face.

He was not a popular attraction; he was just a hamster and no one could be bothered to read the accompanying explanation of what he had done.

Someone tried to make the feature more exciting by dressing him up in a mini Sherlock Holmes costume. Something he had never done whilst he was alive.

---

2. Just to be clear, this isn't the kindest thing you could do for this poor guinea pig. He should have let the guinea pig speak, then given him some dandelion leaves and sent him home. Alas, the vet in this story is a cunt. The owner wasn't much better.
3. Their phone batteries. Physically they weren't particularly tired, they'd only been standing around.

The Internet Part 2
Plants and Succulents

Addicted to gardening Facebook group

Mia Help! This little guy is not doing well. I have no experience with succulents so need some guidance.

Meghan Over watered.

Catherine Over watered.

Don Looks waterlogged to me.

Simone Waterlogged.

Addy Too much water.

Miranda Too much water.

Trevor TOO MUCH WATER.

Brian You've drowned it for some reason???

Mandy Too much water, they don't need much water.

Helen Why have you given it so much water? Were you trying to kill it?

Ian FFS. You've been drowning it.

Becky Too much water, were there no instructions when you bought the plant?

Ken People always just chuck them away without reading.

Becky Yeah, not everyone has green fingers.

Ken It's not about green fingers. It's about know-it-alls.

Helen Probably just bought for Instagram posts.

Ken Well it doesn't look like it's going to come back now.

Ian Needs chucking.

Mia My mum just took off the bottom leaves and it seems alright now.

Ian It won't be.

Diane Here is a picture of my succulent garden. I've been looking after succulents for over 30 years. It takes time and patience to look after these beautiful plants. Something young people today DO NOT HAVE.

Steve Why buy a plant and then take it home and drown it?

Ken Some people just buy them and then let them die and as soon as they go a bit brown; they stick them in the bin along with anything or anyone they don't want anymore. People are DISGUSTING.

Angie Have you tried watering it?

Diane Are you MAD, Angie? I will ask the moderator to remove you if you continue to give bad advice. This young succulent is QUITE CLEARLY OVER WATERED.

Ken This young woman, honestly, she needs a good talking to. Probably been brought up by a single mum. There's no such thing as family anymore. People don't try. People just walk away. Why get married and then just walk away? Why would you just walk away and leave that person behind that you said you loved? Were you not listening in church? It's supposed to be marriage, it's supposed to be UNTIL YOU DIE. What the FUCK is wrong with these slags? Why am I wasting time on a slag that can't even look after a fucking plant.

Mia Are you OK, Ken?

Ken Fuck off, you stupid bitch. I hope you all die.

Marcus Over watered.

Dan Over watered.

Keith Over watered.

Brian Over watered.

Mia Thanks, I realise I've over watered it. I'll stop doing that now.

Carol Over watered.

Hank OVER WATERED.

Jerry Over watered, call yourself a gardener, fuck's sake.

Bea Have you tried watering it?

Dave OVER WATERED YOU FUCKING IMBECILE

Nigel Try moving it to a different window.

Roger Have you tried giving it a bit less water?

Monti Donne

This piece is about an entirely fictional gardener called Monti Donne. Since writing this story it has come to my attention that there is a real and quite well-known gardener with a similar name who seems like a wonderful man. This has nothing to do with him. Just one of those coincidences. Like that time loads of bands called their album 'Best Of'.

I sometimes think about (an entirely fictional) gardener called Monti Donne and his dogs.

What is he doing right now?

Cleaning his tools?

Polishing his spade?

Getting the dirt out of his nails?

Patting his dogs? Or burying them?

Doing some topiary?

Sitting in a deckchair with a hanky over what's left of his curls?

Propagating the soil?

Sowing seeds for the spring?

Scraping the mud from his wellies?

Digging up some potatoes for his dinner?

Making a posy from his jewel garden?
Travelling around the world with his collection of difficult-to-iron linen suits looking at famous gardens?
Having a wank in his potting shed?
Laughing at old videos of his arch-rival the completely sexless Alan Titchmarch?[1]

Does he have a special emoji on his phone to represent Charlie Dimmock's tits for when he's making jokes about her with his vulgar friends?

---

1. Of course, we all know Alan Titchmarsh is incredibly sexy, has lovely big hands (like shovels), and we all love his sexy books and his sexy TV shows. We all want him but we can't have him.

Does he regularly ravish young women who he happens to find wandering lost yet fully aroused in his topiary maze?

Does he always wear a scarf because he's covered in love bites?

I asked around about Monti Donne and it turns out other people have questions.

What is Monti Donne's net worth?

Is Monti Donne ill?

Is Monti Donne's dog ill?

Is Monti Donne's dog dead?

What did Monti Donne's dog die of?

How many dogs does Monti Donne have left?

Does Monti Donne really have hands like shovels?

Does Monti Donne have a son?

How old is Monti Donne's son?

Does Monti Donne's son look anything like Monti Donne?

Does Monti Donne's son also have hands like shovels?

Is Monti Donne a grandfather?

Is that a grandson or a granddaughter that Monti Donne has?

Does it look like Monti Donne's grandson is eventually going to have hands like shovels?

Is it true that Monti Donne gets a semi every time he sees a plant?
Does Monti Donne speak Japanese?
Does Monti Donne speak Korean?
Why does Monti Donne speak Korean?
Does Monti Don have a Korean wife?
Is Monti Donne gay?
Is Monti Donne on Grindr
How active is Monti Donne on Grindr?
How old is Monti Donne's dad?
Is Monti Donne's dad single?
Does Monti Donne's dad have any dogs?
Did Monti Donne inherit his shovel-like hands from his mother or his father?
Does Monti Donne have a favourite tool?
Does Monti Donne have his own range of seeds?
Where can I buy Monti Donne's seed?
Is Monti Donne scared of spiders?
Does Monti Donne have green fingers?
Is Monti Donne really a gardener?
Has Monti Donne ever experimented with drugs?
How many dogs does Monti Donne's dad have?
Is Monti Donne's dad's dog dead?
Is Monti Donne a pensioner?
Does Monti Donne receive a state pension?
Who is Monti Donne's wife?
Does Monti Donne have a happy marriage?
Does Monti Donne do his own gardening?
Does Monti Donne do his own ironing?
Is Monti Donne best friends with Gary Barlow?
Why on earth is Monti Donne best friends with Gary Barlow?
Did Monti Donne audition to be in Take That?
Would Monti Donne be open to having an affair?
How many affairs has Monti Donne had?
Is Monti Donne only attracted to other gardeners?

Does Monti Donne have several mistresses across the globe, all
gardeners?
When did Monti Donne last have an STD test?
What is Monti Donne's favourite plant?
Was Monti Donne in prison?
Why was Monti Donne in prison?
Was Monti Donne in prison with David Dickinson?
What is Monti Donne's favourite food?
Does Monti Donne like spaghetti carbonara?
Why does Monti Donne only eat spaghetti carbonara?
Has Monti Donne ever suffered from rickets?
Is Monti Donne short for Montgomery or Montague or is Monti his
name given at birth?

Why was Monti Donne named Monti Donne at birth?
Has Monti Donne been knighted?
Why has Monti Donne not been knighted?
Does Monti Donne hate the Queen?
Which Queen does Monti Donne hate? Camilla Parker Bowles or the dead one?
Is it true that Monti Donne is a litter bug?
Was Monti Donne fined for dropping litter?
Does Monti Donne fly tip?
Where does Monti Donne fly tip?
Does Monti Donne fly tip in a dogging area?
Is it true Monti Donne has a pile of broken fridges in his garden?
Did someone get trapped inside a fridge and die in Monti Donne's garden?
Has Monti Donne ever been to the South Pole?
Did Monti Donne lose any of his fingers to frostbite?

Did Monti Donne partially lose his nose to frostbite?
Is it true that Monti Donne partially lost his penis to frostbite?
Is it true that Monti Donne only eats meat?
Is Monti Donne from Monte Cristo?
Was Monti Donne in the hit film The Full Monty?
Was the film The Full Monty named after Monti Donne?
Was the Full Monty based on a true story about Monti Donne?
Is Monti Donne still a male stripper?
Is it true that when Monti Donne goes out for breakfast he asks for 'The Full Monty' and then laughs to himself?
Does Monti Donne give out unsolicited autographs?
Does Monti Donne like Monty Python?
Was Monti Donne in Monty Python?

Was Monty Python named after Monti Donne?

Was Monti Donne ever in Spandau Ballet?

Does Monti Donne know Simon Le Bon?

Are Monti Donne and Simon Le Bon related?

Does Simon Le Bon wank in Monti Donne's potting shed?

Do Monti Donne and Simon Le Bon wank in Monti Donne's potting shed?

Does Simon Le Bon have his own potting shed?

Does Yasmin Le Bon know that Simon Le Bon and Monti Donne wank in Monti Donne's potting shed?

Did Monti Donne write a letter to Jon Bon Jovi asking if they might be related, what with their names rhyming and all?

Does Monti Donne have an umbilical hernia?

Once I've worked out the entire back story to this fictional character, I might write a steamy romance about him.

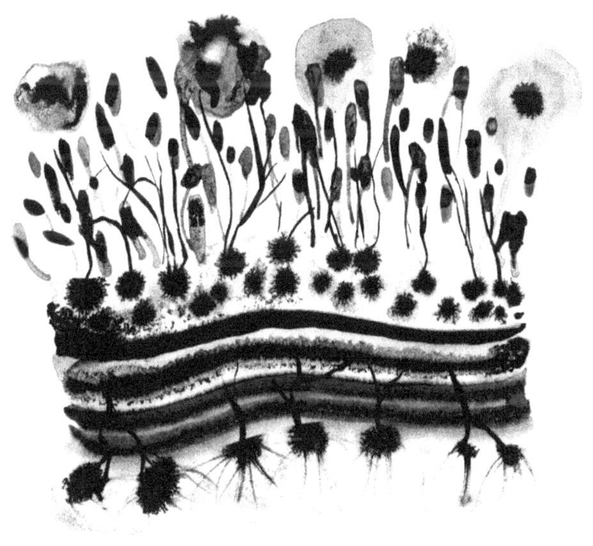

Say Your Prayers

I went into a cathedral with my daughter, and it was so beautiful I decided to try praying; it was quite easy, I just sat down and closed my eyes.

I really enjoyed my first crack at praying. It was a kind of long Christmas list of all the wars that I wanted to end.

Afterwards my daughter told me a woman had seen me praying. I asked her if she thought the woman had seen me praying and believed that I was a woman praying. I wanted to know if I had successfully got into the role of woman praying. Did the woman see me praying and avert her eyes to give me privacy with God? Did she perhaps mistake me for a Catholic?

My daughter didn't know. "She just looked at you for a second, that was it."

I wondered if the woman would go home and tell her family about visiting the cathedral and mention the "praying woman" she had seen.

Perhaps she'd be inspired by my praying to do some praying herself?

Perhaps she thought I looked so serene she would become some sort of religious fundamentalist and have 17 children and marry lots of men and have a big cult and then move to America where that sort of thing is more acceptable.

Was this what the butterfly effect was all about? Had my prayers set off a chain of events that would cause trouble for several centuries?

Would it eventually lead to a religious war?

If so, God really wasn't paying attention because that would be the exact opposite of what I was asking for.

BRIDES AND GROOMS

I saw someone with a copy of *Bride and Groom* magazine and thought, "Wow, that's so niche, a magazine dedicated to people that are OBSESSED with getting married and people that work with horses." I wondered what their readership was, how many subscribers they had and what sort of people chose to advertise in the magazine. I marvelled that they could keep going during the decline of print media.

I decided to flick through it in WHSmith, I couldn't commit to buying a copy. I didn't want the shopkeeper to have a confusing mental image of me and be left wondering if I was really into getting married or really into brushing horses. I know I shouldn't care what people think of me; but I do.

In the back of the magazine, I found adverts for veils and saddle polish. Pointy white shoes and long black boots. Whips for your wedding night for if you want to punish your partner for marrying you or whips for your horses for if you're angry at your horse and want to punish them in a medieval and overtly aggressive way.

They also sold T-shirts for horse lovers that said "I love horses" on them and T-shirts for hen weekends that said "I love cock" on them.

They sold novelty condoms and shire horse semen.

I thought about the person who has to collect the shire horse semen. Do they have to dress up as a horse to be able to arouse the horse or are shire horses sometimes attracted to humans? What sort of humans were they attracted to? Do they have a type? Would they find me attractive? Would they like women who made an effort with their appearance or women that were just nice to them and had kind eyes? Do they like large breasts? Just how superficial were these enormous horses and what led them to be this way?

I started to put search terms into Google which took me down a small but ungodly rabbit hole. Soon I was reading all about selective breeding in animal husbandry and learnt that bull semen is more expensive than gold.

I wondered if I had room in the garden for a bull and I could give up work and just wank off a pet bull every day. I wondered if I would have to do this wearing a cow costume. I wondered if bulls have a type of cow they are more attracted to, was udder size a factor?

I started to google cow costumes. I found one on eBay that had been used in a pantomime. It needs two people to wear it. I wondered if I'd go in the front or the back. I wondered which friend would want to go into business with me.

I wondered if the bull would actually mount the pantomime cow and if we'd be strong enough to take its weight whilst decanting the semen into some sort of suitable receptacle inside the cow costume. How big would the bottle need to be? Would we need to wear dry robes inside the suit so we didn't get drenched? Or perhaps a wet suit would be better for the job?

I wondered if I would need to dress as a matador at any point in the process. I decided yes.

I vaguely wondered if there were any rules about keeping bulls in suburbia but thought I had perhaps seen something on *The Good Life*[1] about keeping a bull or two in your back garden.

I wondered if all this would disgruntle my neighbours, and then realised I could time it so that we don't enter the garden in the pantomime cow costume until they've gone to work.

But what if they come back early? I worried a little and then decided it really isn't any of their fucking business.

I went back to WHSmith to look for a magazine that would be good for advertising my bull semen in. I found a good one called *Gardening and Seamen*.

Unfortunately, on closer inspection, it was about gardening and sailors with absolutely no mention of animal husbandry.

There were some good adverts in the back though for seeds and white flared trousers, miniature rose bushes and all sorts of nautically themed home décor.

I didn't commit to buying a copy though, because I didn't want the shop keeper to think I was on leave from the royal navy... Or that I was OBSESSED with gardening more than is normal for an adult woman. I know I shouldn't care what people think of me, but I do.

I decided to take a closer look at the seed section to see if you could buy seamen seed. I'd often thought of having a child... I threw some search terms into Google and once again went down an ungodly rabbit hole.

---

1. A very important documentary from the 1970's about self-sufficiency.

SERENITY

Today I reached my ideal weight, but it's taken me so many years I no longer have the ideal face to go with it.

Annoying.

There was a time when I had the ideal face and the ideal weight at the same time but I didn't have the ideal brain to go with it, so I was unaware.

Also annoying.

I start googling Jowl Watchers to see if I can pay a monthly subscription to go to a meeting of like-minded individuals who want to do something about their jowls, perhaps someone there could measure my jowls? Perhaps there would be an app as well as a regular meeting and I could update the app on how my jowls were on any given day.

"I've had a bad week; my jowls seem longer than ever."

I would go to the front of the class and get my jowls measured. I wouldn't have lost or gained. I would get a round of applause.

Someone at the back would be clapping but silently furious that my jowls were not as big as theirs and yet I was making a big deal of it.

A rumour would spread around the group. Someone tried to trick the system by gluing their jowls to their ears.

Someone else had not been seen at the group but was suspected of breaking rank and having cheap jowl surgery in Turkey.

Someone joined the group who was only 25 and they were universally loathed, but it did bring the rest of the group together in their hatred.

Marcel

I liked Marcel Marceau very much.

Everything about him really.

He had a simple style and he didn't talk.

He had a great body, was expressive but mostly quiet.

I like quiet. Some people just talk too much.

My husband talked too much.

He had many, many, unwavering opinions on things he knew very little about.

He talked loudly so he would drown me out.

He wore salmon-coloured jeans and his shirts were so loud they were bordering on aggressive.

And I dreamt of Marcel.

A quiet man, a quiet lover, who would move beautifully, and quietly.

Marcel would never grunt in my ear.

He would pluck a rose from nowhere and present it to me with no words.

He would not need a long speech of gratitude for the rose; a nod, a smile, a hand on my heart would be enough. And then we could go on being quiet.

So, on Monday I emptied out my husband's wardrobe whilst he was out playing squash. I replaced his many shirts with 20 black and white striped long sleeve black tops. All identical. I replaced his trousers with black leggings with braces attached. His trainers with simple black pumps.

On Tuesday I replaced his Nivea for Men with thick white foundation.

On Wednesday I painted the entire house in shades of black and grey and white.

I took down his *Pulp Fiction* posters and popped them in the recycling. They had been up for so long the Blu Tac was not salvageable.

On Thursday, Friday and Saturday I observed his confusion.

And on Sunday I ripped out his vocal cords.

BLACK PUDDING

I went out and overheard a girl talking in a pub garden. She told the people at her table that she made black pudding from what she poured out of her moon cup. Her friends didn't believe her; she insisted she did, that it was good for her, that it was just like eating a placenta. She said that since she'd been doing it, she no longer had an iron deficiency. Her friends asked her if she couldn't have just gone to Holland and Barrett?

I thought about Scott of the Antarctic and Captain Oates and how they could have survived using this new semi-acceptable version of cannibalism if only they were menstruating women and not over-reaching Edwardian men.

I thought about Scott of the Antarctic and Captain Oates and how if they'd have been alive today, they would wear North Face jackets, run to work every day in leggings for absolutely no reason and do triathlons and ultra-marathons and not see their kids much.

What a pair of wankers.

LADYBIRD RESCUE

I just rescued a ladybird from a bucket of water.

It looked like it had already accepted its fate.

I pulled it back from the brink.

Having been so close to death, will this ladybird be changed?

Will it start helping out other ladybirds?

Will it finally start trying to do its dream job?

Will it care less about things and spend more time with its friends, family and children?

Will it start donating a huge percentage of its wages to charity?

Will it become altruistic?

Did it have a conversation with God?

Was I the answer to its prayers?

Did some giant unseen hand push me towards the bucket of water and make me spy the little red circling dot?

Did it then push me to bend down and intervene?

I don't normally look in buckets of rainwater.

I don't usually go out of my way to save insects.

Will the ladybird now look at the rest of its life as the time after the bucket and look back at the time before the bucket and cringe and shake its head and not believe what it used to be like?

Will it have more faith in humans now?

Will it stick around and try and do a good turn for me?

Will it start boring people about what it used to be like and how it's a much better person now?

Will it get an agent and start doing the public speaking circuit?

Talking about grabbing life whilst you can because it can all be gone in an instant?

Will it have its own range of merchandise with inspirational quotes on it?

"Be the change you want to see in the world."

"If not now, when?"

"Kindness makes your face beautiful."

"The best time to act is now."

Will it start doing fucking triathlons to raise money for charity?

Will it rearrange its spots so they spell out North Face across its back?

What hell had I unleashed on the world?

I went back outside; the ladybird was still there, walking around and presumably trying to dry off fully before attempting to fly.

I curled my fingers and flicked it into the air.

I hoped this would make it less of a sanctimonious cunt.

TODAY IN THE SAUNA

I listened to a man enthuse with real passion about his nine-year-old grandson who he said has taught himself fluent Chinese, Japanese, French, Spanish, Urdu and Mandarin from his phone. I say he sounds amazing.

I'm a bit sceptical to be honest about the actual fluency of this kid but who am I to judge?

I just wonder how they know he's fluent.

I ask if there are people in the family that speak these languages and he said, 'No.'

Has the grandfather taken him to meet people who speak these languages to test it out? Might the kid just be speaking jibberish with the rest of the family watching him and nodding proudly?

My inner monologue tells me off for being cynical and mean. Sometimes my inner monologue expects more from me than I am able to achieve.

I WENT TO HOLLYWOOD

I went to Hollywood and got my tits, lips and arse pumped up. I had lash extensions and got a brand-new set of teeth.

Then I flew back to Bury and went to Greggs for a pastie and a custard doughnut.

I caught sight of myself in St Ann's Hospice shop window. I liked my new shape but I was covered in pastie crumbs.

I was unsure what to do next with my life.

BIBLE STUDIES

Today in the sauna there was a young man who had just finished his bible studies degree and was now hoping to become an RE teacher. He asked me if I was spiritual. I never know what to say with these types of questions, I don't want to cause offence, I don't want to shit on someone's beliefs, and if I say YES who knows what he might tell me? If I say NO will the conversation close down? I don't believe in GOD but thinking about the universe and looking at the night sky terrifies me. Does that make me spiritual?

I make the decision.

"Yes, I'm *really* spiritual."

He tells me he loves Hebrew poetry and in particular an acrostic.

I was surprised at this. I have been moved by lots of different types of writing, but never an acrostic.

It made me think about being at primary school, being introduced to the concept of writing a poem where the first letter of each line had to form a word.

I wrote my acrostic using the word Zena. I still have it in a box in my best child's handwriting mounted on faded red paper.

ZENA

Z - Zebras are basically horses with stripes that no one can ride, I don't know why we don't just call them stripey horses and be done with it.
E - Elephants are grey and apparently remember everything, but I don't see how we can truly know this.
N - Newts are quite hard to catch and no one knows if they remember everything or not.
A - Anteaters only eat ants, they must despise teatime.

I asked him if he could recite his favourite acrostic to me but he couldn't remember it. I said that was understandable, being put on the spot is never easy. He said the main gist of the acrostic is that "Life is Vapour".

I nodded. That sounds wise. The other people in the sauna nodded too. Yes, we all nodded. Life is vapour.

I then had to leave the sauna because I was too hot and the air in there is very dry.

ORNITHOLOGY

Today I decided to get into ornithology.
I spotted a dead cuckoo in my garden. "Aha!" I thought to myself. It's him that's been spitting all over my plants. I have always found spitting repugnant behaviour so I happily offered

up the body of the cuckoo to my cat after first checking the body for signs of rabies.

I realised I didn't know what to look for, rabies-wise, but couldn't see anything untoward.

My cat has led an easy life though, so had no interest in the body.

Luckily the magpies spotted it and they tucked in after a bit of a tussle over it.

Magpies are absolute cunts aren't they? No respect, no solidarity. And to think people bother to salute to them when they have no appreciation of nice manners.

I decided to get into cooking birds instead as part of my foray into ornithology and went for the difficult medieval bird-in-a-bird option.[1] I stuffed a sparrow into a pigeon and then the pigeon into a chicken and then a chicken into a swan. It wasn't easy getting the swan in the oven.[2] I had to pull most of its feathers off and its wings. I was going to use the feathers to stuff my cushions with but on closer inspection they were full of mites.

---

1. It's called Turducken, usually a chicken inside a duck inside a turkey. I don't understand this as they are similar sized birds. It should be more like the woman who swallowed a fly and then a series of animals that get larger. Although it's an awful lot of death for one meal TBH. I certainly don't have the stomach for it.

2. It is illegal to kill swans and eat them unless you're Camilla Parker Bowles. She's allowed to do what she wants with them. I think she mainly watches them from a safe distance.

I contacted the local ornithology Facebook group with photos of my dinner and told them about the cunt magpies and they blocked me.

No wonder people are put off from taking up these pursuits. It's such a closed shop. Fuck them. I'm going to have a crack at archaeology instead; or metal detecting, or cheese rolling.

Maybe I'll find my own peat bog man,[3] I'd like to see their faces when I show them that.

---

3.   A peat bog man is a man that has been found in some peat. He's usually dead and a few thousand years old with well-preserved leathery skin and a chiselled jawline (think Tom Jones or Des O'Connor).

Nails

Today in the sauna there was a woman in there with a small bag of toiletries. She unzipped it. Took out nail clippers and starting cutting her toenails. They pinged onto the floor. There was no one else in there to look at and do a shocked / amused / disgusted raised eyebrow face at so I left.

We all have our limits and I couldn't tell if she had a hernia so there was nothing to look at other than the hard yellow shards on the tiled floor.

THE INTERNET PART 3
PUPPY TRAINING

New Puppy Owners Advice and Support Group

Chloe Can anyone help me? My dog hasn't been going on the potty much and licks her private area what should I do about it? Any advice? Thanks

Ian Why are you putting your dog on a potty? What's wrong with you?

Rosie My dog did that before I had her spayed, how old is she? Could she be in season?

Catherine Why are you watching your dog lick herself?

Duncan Why are you putting your dog on a potty? What breed is your dog? Not that any breeds should be trained with a potty. They need to go outside. They're not babies.

Mary My dog died last year.

Denise Why on earth have you tried to put your dog on a potty? No wonder she's distressed.

Angela Why are you watching your dog do her private business? Do you enjoy people watching you on the toilet?

Sam SHE PROBABLY DOES

Moira Is she on heat?

Chloe Oh yes, it could be that. I'll have to go and get her spayed. The vet did say I should bring her in after she's been in season at least once. Does anyone know how long a season usually lasts?

Sam It's fucking irresponsible to not spay your dog FFS. This group.

Denise You really must spay your dog. Sorry to hear about your dog Mary. Why did she die?

Claude SPAY YOUR DOG

Margaret SPAY YOUR FUCKING DOG

Mary It was her kidneys. I've been heartbroken ever since.

Denise You probably fed her the wrong type of food Mary. Unfortunately, you can't keep giving them treats. You probably killed her, no offence.

Mary She loved a bit of ice cream.

Denise There you go, Mary, you killed her. You can stay on this group if you like, but if you try and offer advice I'll have to report you because you obviously have no idea how to care for a canine. No offence.

Dan   It's not fair to your dog not to spay her, she will get followed by dogs when you take her out and they can't help it. They can't help it at all. You can't blame them for doing what comes naturally. It's instinctual. They need the release you see. If a dog has full balls and doesn't empty them once in a while it's very bad for the dog, it gets very uncomfortable. And then they see your wee puppy and god help her. But it's not the dog's fault, I repeat NOT THE DOGS FAULT. It's the bitch's fault.

Ange   Get her spayed and then she won't get followed by other dogs.

Dan   She might still get followed but it's less likely a dog will mount her and attempt sexual intercourse.

Duncan   She's probably starting her own puppy farm and coming on here for medical advice because she's too selfish to pay for the vets.

Angela   Urgh, people are disgusting.

Dan   Chloe, I've sent you a friend request, why haven't you accepted?

Chloe   Sorry, I don't know you.

Dan   You do know me, I've been telling you how to look after your puppy!!!!!!!!

Chloe   I only friend people I know in real life.

Dan   FUCKING BITCH LIKE YOUR DOG

THE LIFT MAN

There is a man in a London hotel who has worked the lift for 30 years. He has dedicated his life to going up and down. Pressing the button for people because they are too posh to push their own button. I would like to ask him:

Does he go up and down in his dreams?

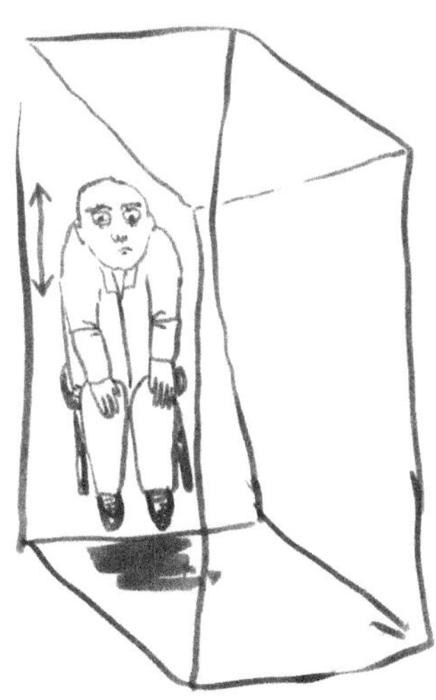

Are all his dreams lift based?

Does he prefer going up or down?

How many times in the 30 years has he been stuck?

What is the worst thing anyone has ever said to him whilst being in the lift?

Does he feel after 30 years he knows everything there is to know about the lift?

Do his feet feel wobbly when he takes a break?

I presume he doesn't eat his sandwiches in the lift. It's a posh hotel and that sort of thing would be frowned upon.

I like his dedication to doing one thing well. I wonder if he always fancied doing it as a child.

If we all did one thing, the one thing that we were best at, would the world be a better place? What would I do? Would we be happier? But I am not an interviewer. I have no access to the man, I don't know his name or which hotel he works in. So, I will have to guess the answers:

Sometimes.

No.

Up.

23.

"Press the fucking button then."

Not really.

No.

No, of course he doesn't eat his sandwiches in the lift.

No, he never wanted to do it as a child, don't be so fucking patronising.

PRIDE AND PREJUDICE

I was proud of myself but embarrassed about my foreign dog.

This Morning in the Sauna

The whole gang was there, the lovely vicar, the car mechanic, the man who had been attacked by a shark whilst visiting his son in Australia, the man who brings in punnets of strawberries, the retired nurse, the PR woman, the retired chef and the man who talks a lot about bridge and billiards. Now that everyone knows the lovely vicar is a vicar the course of the conversation has changed. It feels like an off-shoot confessional for godless triers. Somehow we all look to him to lead the conversation and one by one we tell him about our plans for the weekend.

I don't have weekend plans, so I tell the vicar I've been thinking about getting a greenhouse, but I'm worried about disturbing sleeping hedgehogs. (I wanted to appear kind to animals because I presume vicars like that sort of shit). Everyone chimed in that I would have to wait until spring for my greenhouse. Shark attack man chimed in that I would lose propagation time if I waited until spring. In my head I was counting the cost of the hedgehogs' lives against the 20% sale on greenhouses ending. I didn't mention the financial element though. Realistically, I could never hurt a hedgehog, even if they threw in free delivery and set up.

One lady has a school reunion. she hasn't seen them for 39 years, which is an unsatisfying number in that they should have waited for the big four zero, but then at least the number 39 divides into 3 and I like that in a number, and whilst 40 is a round number, it's almost too round? Too horrible? The number 4 is no number 2, is it? As numbers go, I'd just say this... it's unpleasant.

I wonder how long she is intending to sit in the sauna? Is she trying to quickly go down a couple of dress sizes before the big reunion? I've heard that can work, although if you drink water at the same rate as sweating probably not. And no one wants to go to a school reunion as a raisin, it's probably not a good idea. I ask her if there will be anyone there that she hates and she replies, "Them lot aren't invited." "Ah that's good," I say, there's always a "them lot" and they're always cunts.

The vicar is going on a team building weekend with other vicars. Apparently, a lot of meditation followed by a pub quiz. I hope they all wear their little outfits for the pub quiz. I would find that quite charming, despite not being a fan of religion. I suppose no one is a fan of religion really, people don't say things like "I like reading books, listening to music and religion". It's not like that. I wonder what music I would choose if I could only pick one band. I'd probably say none at all, because it would get too annoying after a while. I wonder if that's what religion is like. Starts off exciting and then becomes annoying because it's always the same thing? Someone should write a new chapter to the Bible. Maybe I'll do that next. Maybe one day people will view this book as a sort of bible.

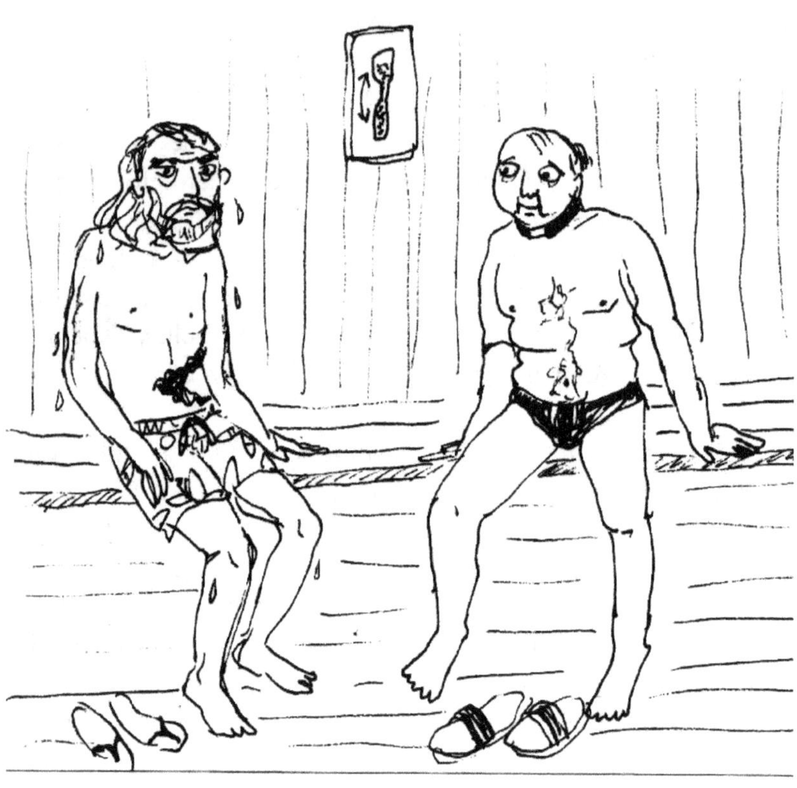

THE WOODS

"I went to the woods because I wished to live deliberately, to front only the essential facts of life, and see if I could not learn what it had to teach, and not, when I came to die, discover that I had not lived. I did not wish to live what was not life, living is so dear; nor did I wish to practise resignation, unless it was quite necessary. I wanted to live deep and suck out all the marrow of life, to live so sturdily and Spartan-like as to put to rout all that was not life, to cut a broad swath and shave close, to drive life into a corner, and reduce it to its lowest terms..." — Henry David Thoreau

Inspired by Henry David Thoreau I decided to follow in his footsteps. I googled to see where the nearest woods were. They were only about a 20-minute drive away.

I didn't have a National Trust card though, so the parking was £7 just for one day. This would be no good, because I wanted to live in the woods, I needed to park my car permanently, or until I decided to stop sucking the marrow out of life.

I asked the man at the booth how long it would be for a month and he said that wasn't a possibility.

I told him I had come to the woods to live and he said I couldn't, that someone owned the woods and I wasn't allowed to live there.

I asked him how this person had come to own the woods?

He wasn't sure.

I said all property is theft.

He said if my car was still there after 6pm it would get clamped.

I said I'd take a one-hour ticket, unpack all my gear, carry it into the woods, then drive my car home and then get a bus back.

He said I wasn't allowed to leave things in the woods.

I said I'd be tidy, that I wouldn't make a big imprint on the woods, that I wanted to live frugally, that I just wanted to suck the marrow out of life.

He said I beg your pardon.

I said I'd bury my poo and respect the woods.

He said he would have to call the police if I didn't move along.

I said I did not wish to live what was not life.

He said he was picking up the phone.

I got back in my car and drove home.

I unpacked everything.

I was exhausted.

I made a nice cup of tea and watched some television.

I had hoped to be busy looking for a natural source of water.

I had hoped to be busy capturing rain water from the trees with plastic bottles I had repurposed.

I had hoped to be foraging for wild fungus that I could fry up on a camp fire.

I had hoped to be building a small but sturdy shelter using only what I could find in my immediate surroundings.

I had hoped to have captured a couple of rats and skinned them and roasted them over a small campfire that I would also use for purifying water. I checked my book.

"I wanted to live deep and suck out all the marrow of life, to live so sturdily and Spartan-like as to put to rout all that was not life, to cut a broad swath and shave close, to drive life into a corner, and reduce it to its lowest terms..."

There was a knock on the door. It was the kids back from school. I would have to check on my iCal to see if there was another day I could fit in some time to suck the marrow out of life. I thought perhaps I could roll it out to the corporate world as a team-building exercise. I opened a spreadsheet and began to plan and then fixed a time to meet with a possible investor.

CAKE

In the sauna this evening someone was sharing round pieces of birthday cake. I knew it was wrong, to eat cake in the sauna, but joined in anyway and took a piece. It wasn't very nice, but I had to eat it because there are no food wastebins in the sauna. I will try and remember to ask them at the front desk to put a bin in there. And maybe a small dustpan and shovel for the nail clippings. And come to think of it maybe a microwave so we can warm up our lunch/dinner before taking it into the sauna to eat. And perhaps a kettle if we want to make gravy to go on the dinner.

Also, perhaps they could have a shelf with a few basic items we would use, salt and pepper, gravy granules, a variety of spices, some dried lentils, a slow cooker, a blender and fresh eggs. Perhaps a small hob for frying bacon?

Tiny Head

I went to the doctor about my tiny head. We googled the symptom together and couldn't find any treatments that didn't sound incredibly dangerous. I wasn't completely sure she was a real doctor. She asked me if I wanted antidepressants or an inhaler. I didn't.

She said when I got home I should rummage in my cupboards and just "see what I had".

As I headed for the door she shouted after me, "Try juicing and mindfulness."

CHINA

Today in the sauna there was a tall and muscular Adonis sat on the top step. Imagine Michelangelo's David come to life but without the catapult. He was in the sauna reading a very thick book called simply *China*. It was the size of one of those books in the library that you have to ask a librarian to get down for you and then lay it on a table and then wear special gloves to turn the pages.

A wizard's 500-year-old book.

The size of book you could kill a man with if you brought it down with force. Have you got the picture now? It was a big ridiculous fucking book, OK? [1]

He was not wearing special gloves. In fact, he had wet hands, the pages would get pulpy.

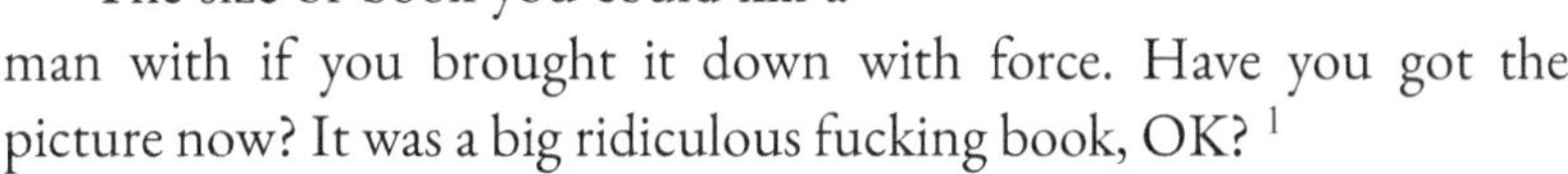

1. The image you see here doesn't really show you the true scale of the size of the book. Also, the man in question didn't have his dick out, it's not that type of sauna.

The Adonis was only about three pages into his thousand-page book about China. I wondered how far he would get through the book before having to leave and then carry his big book back to the changing rooms.

I didn't have to wonder for long... He got to page four.

It was a fucking stupid book to take to the gym.

ACID REFLUX

Today in the sauna there was a man talking to another man about his acid reflux.

A quick scan[1] of their bodies told me they had no hernias, umbilical or other.

Man 1 said to Man 2 that he was about to embark on a diet.

In fact he said that he had just been diagnosed with a bad heart condition, but he had watched a video on YouTube that said his heart condition could be fixed by only eating meat. So, he was going to do that, even though he would find it hard.

He said, "We are meat eaters after all, carnivores, you know." He tapped his fang teeth.

I shot a glance to the other woman on the top step of the sauna.

She arched her eyebrow at me and smiled but looked down.

I had learnt not to get involved with men's medical conditions.

---

1. I don't have x-ray vision like Superman / Supergirl. I scanned them with my eyes.

Archaeology

The year is 9875 and a small team of archaeologists are working their way through layers of dirt to find the remains of the people that lived around the era of 2000-2050. They want to try and work out what happened, where it went so wrong.

Before we almost wiped ourselves out entirely.

They crack open rocks and inside them, where once we found amenities, they find pedometers.

People enjoy going down to Dorset to hunt for phone chargers.

Regular Life

'Twas the Regular Life Christmas party, and as Christmas parties went, it was extremely regular. Picture an open-plan office, sweat patches, desks with teddies on them, swivel chairs, passive-aggressive notices and computers with gonks stuck to them. The ceiling was made of those polystyrene tiles. The carpet was also tiled so when people spilt their tea they could replace just one tile. But no one ever bothered to actually do that so the whole thing was covered in years and years of tea stains.

The party involved having some wine from one of the cups from the water cooler. They installed the water cooler because everyone had forgotten how to use the tap in the kitchen.

Some people had put tinsel on their desks.

50% of the staff hoped to retire soon to spend more time on the sofa, bringing on type 2 diabetes in front of the television.

They also hoped to occasionally see their grandchildren and give them gifts they neither wanted nor needed from pensions that they worked for by spending 30 years sitting in a swivel chair talking about diets/golf under harsh lighting.

The other 50% wished they worked at More-Than-Just-Your-Regular-Life up the road. They sold similar products but had a slide installed in the office that went from the 4th floor all the way to the 3rd floor. It was installed by a wacky manager they'd had there in the 90's.

The people that worked at More-Than-Just-Your-Regular-Life were too embarrassed to go on it. They pretended to be uninterested. It was only ever mentioned when they told people about their job. "We have a slide," they would say, and the people they told would be jealous.

At the Regular Life Christmas party two colleagues were having a very limp romance that would conclude with a wedding in a small castle where the ladies would clip feathers to their hair in order to appear fascinating. They would have two acceptable children followed by a typical divorce.

The only person that truly was fascinating was Carol, who had her leg amputated in Turkey in order to lose weight after eating too much turkey. She instantly lost two stone but then put it all back on during a difficult and painful recovery.

Everything is Made
of Soil

I used to think, that one day I would be a pretty significant person. I never knew quite how. My only talent that could potentially set me apart from everyone else is the ability to make my ears make a popping sound and to have very bendy arms. This was never going to get me very far in life. Some people are maths geniuses or have music in their fingertips. I just have bendy arms. I've never been able to make a living from it and I suspect I never will.

It's fine, I've accepted my fate and am trying to make the best of it. I am not one of the Stephen Hawkings or George Michaels of this world, but I do have a party trick I can do on demand. Did they? (Yes, I know I know, singing and doing maths and whatnot, fair enough.)

I have accepted my fate as one of life's not-significant-people, and it feels OK. I now know that even the best of us just trend on Twitter for a few hours or make the news if we've done something really special, and then what?

We don't get to hear of our death on the news or the local paper… We don't get to hear the speeches. If we live long enough, no one will be alive who cares or remembers us. We'll be desperate to die to get away from all the bloody people talking to us in a loud baby voice. As our skin gets thinner and starts to hang from our body, when no one wants to touch us anymore, we are devalued to just being some old person who has the audacity to still be alive. So many parts of us will already be gone.

Even now, in middle age, friends have died, and each of them took a piece of me with them. They didn't mean to, they just did.

They are no longer here to confirm or deny our shared history. If I don't tell anyone about it, did it ever happen? If I forget things, there is no one around to remind me of it, it's gone for good. If I change the story, no one can prove it. When their life flashed before them in their final moments, was I in the slide show? Did I make the cut? Popping my ears and bending my arms at school? Some memory they had about me has gone into the grave with them. That memory became liquid. Then soil. Indistinguishable now from anything else but made from memories. Sorry to make this about me, but I'm having an existential crisis here, can't you tell?

Look at the trees in graveyards. Fertilised by the bodies underneath them. Are their trunks filled with the DNA of the dead? Does every leaf know something you don't? Something they cannot repeat. Do they know anything about me? Have they seen me naked? They might have. They might know me better than anyone else. Thank goodness trees can only communicate with other trees. How far have they spread the gossip? Has the news of my bendy arms made its way to the Amazon rain forest through a complicated system of roots? How far do roots go? Can they cross oceans?

Once we are dead, any stories that are told about us won't be for our ears. If someone secretly loved us, loathed us or, even worse, was indifferent to us, we will never know... Ask them now!

Do you secretly love me?

Oh.

Do you loathe me?

Do you feel indifferent towards me?

Ah, I see.

Thank you for that information.

Or does that just make things awkward?

A cemetery opens early and holds cremation after cremation after cremation all day long. Friends and family walk in the front and leave weeping through the back.

Every family walks in with a CD of the greatest hits of Frank Sinatra. "Could you play 'That's Life' on the way in and 'I Did it My Way' on the way out please?"

And did you? Did you do it *your* way? Was it *very* different? Was it? How different could it possibly be? You probably still slept and got up, did your morning ablutions and then got on with your day, earnt some money to pay for food and then went to bed later on. Am I right?

Perhaps I am psychic, maybe I have a special skill after all.

What song will get chosen for me? I hope there is an interpretive dance to go with it. I'd like everyone to wear flesh-coloured body suits and neutral masks. Push back the pews and really make the space their own. Have some mushrooms and get catatonic whilst my body burns… That's something I wouldn't mind watching. Damnit.

We are yellow-spined dog-eared books on a shelf. We are fading photographs in a box if we ever even got printed, and if no one wrote a name on the back of those photos, we are a nameless person from the past, look at our funny hair! You may have been carefully stuck into a photograph album but someone will chuck you away eventually when they have absolutely no idea who you were.

We are an anecdote that changes every time until it's not told anymore.

We are a ghost on the internet. Google us and we are still there. We've just been inactive for a very long time. We'll be stored on some outdated computer system in a basement somewhere and when that technology fails, as it is as infallible as us, it will take our last ghostly internet imprints with it.

Break us down to our elements and we are, at most, a bucket of blood, an unsightly mound of streaky bacon. A pile of bones. Some gristle.

We are all skeletons covered in tracksuits that buy birdfeeders so we can watch the birds, watch the beautiful birds from our kitchen window whilst we cook the birds, eat the birds and scrape the remains of the birds into the bin.

We are so deluded we wear clothes with skeletons painted on them. Entirely forgetting about the skeleton that lies beneath our clothes, an inch behind a layer of meat.

OK, maybe more than an inch.

We are blood, pints and pints of blood swashing around a skeleton, covered with a layer of lard and skin, half the time just lying unconscious on a mattress.

But oh, we think we're really something. Admit it. You're probably thinking, "Well, maybe *she's* nothing because all she can do is pop her ears, but it's not like that for me, I can do 50 squats and am excellent at paintball."

No one cares.

We get on planes and go to other countries and park our walking butchers' shop on the beaches and we lightly cook ourselves as our hugely anticipated annual recreation.

Let's all sit in a sandpit with strangers and change colour. Then go back to work and say, "Oooh yes, I had a lovely time changing colour, I saved all year so I could fly off and sit in a sandpit and change colour, are you going away soon? Which sandpit are you going to? Ooh lovely, you'll really change colour when you go there, my mate went there and you wouldn't believe how much she changed colour and she said the sandpit was lovely."

We are all skeletons wearing sequins to disguise the blood and meat and bones.

We spend our lives collecting things that are all made of ... soil... and that one day ... will be soil again. Just like we will. Just like parts of us already are. We're already halfway there.

We live in the vain hope of leaving something behind. Some memory of us. That we were, here. Against all the odds and all the evidence.

Even though, we remember Jesus and Judas. 2000 years ago, the good man and the bad man. Then we don't remember anyone else until Shakespeare. And then if you're honest who do you remember? Samuel Pepys? The man who wrote a diary whilst his street burnt down?

Napoleon? Some French dude with one arm? Or was that Nelson? One of them has a column, one of them has one eye, I know that much. So fucking what?

We will not be remembered, that is the truth of it. And everything we own will turn back into soil via the charity shop.

We are blood and meat and bones in blue jeans. And we judge each other on the type of jeans we wear to cover up all of the meat we're trying to hide underneath.

We are hair and teeth and nails and we wear fake hair, fake teeth, fake nails trying to disguise our decay. Our journey back to the ground. No one wants to look like the aged animal they are.

We are rejection. The first pieces set out their stall and build a base camp. By the time we are forty the walls are high, with guards and lookouts and warning signals, a sentry sits there with buckets of burning oil to fling when necessary. They hit the air and turn into self-deprecating jokes as they land. We have to use the jokes. Burning oil is not socially acceptable, even if you smile whilst you pour it.

That collection you have? The one you've spent 30 years on? Porcelain pigs from all over the world? Your children hate them. They will give them away with delight. They will get broken and separated in the charity shop. A child will walk in and buy part of your collection with their 50 pence pocket money. The pig will go in their toy box. It will get broken. The mother will be glad it's broken, it is not to her taste, and she will gleefully throw the sharp pieces into the bin. One less bit of tat to look at. I know this to be true, I bought one fancy spoon from someone's beloved fancy spoon collection and then put it in the dishwasher. It's a utilitarian spoon now. The owner would turn in their grave if they weren't already liquid. They'd shout, "Don't separate my fancy spoon collection, that's my life's work you mother fucker!" Perhaps the trees are silently screaming this whenever I walk past them. I hope not, I hope they don't hold grudges in their branches. They should learn to get over it.

We are humiliation, we are a silo of every humiliation that ever took place in our lives. We store it for a lifetime. We keep the lid on tight because if we lose the lid, or anything spills out. we feel all of it and no one wants it, no one wants to be around it. No one wants to feel *that*. We can't even watch people on the television being humiliated, or be about to be humiliated. We have to watch from behind a pillow. At least I do. Has it ended yet? We don't want to see it in case we feel it with them. We store it for a lifetime, an unwelcome visitor we can't get rid of.

We date, and we talk and laugh and pretend we're interested in a thousand different things. He looks nice, he likes red wine (but not too much red wine), reading books (but nothing you'd buy in a supermarket), making nice meals from *The River Cottage Cookbook* and going for long walks. He's disguised all of his meat underneath a nice jumper. He's no stranger to a William Morris pattern and he doesn't look violent, sounds like a keeper!

But do we know what we actually care about? Really? I like politics, but mostly for the tittle tattle. Is it the drama that I like? Is it politicians being humiliated? Am I *that* person? Oh, come on, we are ALL that person? Given the chance, would I be prisoner-turned-lunatic guard? I'm probably not as nice as I think I am. Be warned.

We are all those bits of Tupperware from takeaways when you couldn't be bothered to cook... Oh no ... you won't cook because this pile of blood and meat and bones wants to be waited on. This is a lazy pile of meat. And what was that you say? You want to order what? Oh, just some other meat to stuff in your body made of meat. In fact, three different kinds of meat. So you sit there pushing ducks and chickens and cows down your human meaty throat. And then you fall asleep because when human meat needs to digest cows and pigs and ducks, it takes time. And we keep cats and dogs as pets and feed them on chickens and cows and fish all mushed up together and pressed into pretty shapes.

We are really, really weird.

And when we see people on holiday. Lying on the beach, getting pink in the sun and showing off their rolls of meat that had hitherto been disguised, we hold our noses. Do we want to be reminded of all of that ... skin ... that flesh ... that meat. Is that what we look like? Is that what we are? Am I really just a barrel of blood? I feel like I am more... But probably not. We've been tricked into thinking we are more. Evolution has really fucked us up. Those chimps at Chester Zoo look happy, why can't we just do what they do? I wouldn't mind the cage so long as it was big enough and electric blankets could be made available ... and good internet connection of course; oh, and I suppose I'd like my thumbs to be opposable if possible, so I can still play thumb wars.

We walk around shedding cells, so many there is a constant storm taking place around us. The Great Shedding. We leave pieces of us behind on everything we touch. We spend a lifetime filling our brains, striving to be better. We try to fill ourselves up with all the best stuff, read the best books, eat the good food, speak to the right people. We pride ourselves on having good brains that make fast connections.

It takes three minutes to empty out a lifetime of knowledge. For it to turn to mush. To liquid. To water. To something we wouldn't eat. Those connections we were so proud of? All that time at university ... all of that trying and failing and succeeding and failing again. Of love and loss and getting over that pain and grief and tears and expansion ... of getting fit and getting fat and getting fit again. Of falling out and falling in and glowing up and growing out and growing down.

It's all gone.

Any secrets you held you finally release. They are liquid now. If someone found one, they wouldn't be able to decipher it.

We are made of blood and meat and bones, all of us, but we pride ourselves on our differences.

There are no differences.

We are all just trying.

We are all just pretending.

Passing the time until we are soil again

And who knows what we'll come back as? Maybe if we're lucky we'll be a tree next time. Much less frantic, more longevity, we would get better with age, we would be around to see what happens and we wouldn't go grey. Then someone will come along and chop us down and make us into a bed. And have sex on us and sleep on us not knowing that the bed they lie on is full of human remains that once held secrets and told lies and sung in the car and ate meat and lived a life and died a death.

And that bed will fall apart and it will go to the tip and a seagull will land on us and we will not know and no one will care.

You give your baby toasted soldiers made with bread made from wheat grown on ancient battlefields and wonder why he cries at night.

Someone visits you and says, "Your baby has wise eyes." In fact, you all agree he has wise eyes. "That one's been here before," someone else says. And you all nod in agreement. And even though you are a rational person, you think yes, my baby has lived many times before and holds an unimaginable store of wisdom, never mind that he screams all night, he is the oracle.

And of course he has been here before, and you have, and I have, bits of us have been here since the beginning of time. You've probably been an iceberg and passed through the body of Christ in the form of a fish... And then your wise oracle baby needs his nappy changing. Because for now, he is piss and shit and meat and blood and bones and so are you and so am I and so are we all.

But can I ask one thing of you? If you meet me, ask me to pop my ears for you, ask me to bend my arms? Let me have my moment in the sunshine. Be amazed at the popping sound. Be astounded at how far up my back my arms will go. Let me impress you, let me feel what it's like to be Beyoncé for just one little moment, probably in some Manchester pub garden. Not that Beyoncé would pop her ears and show off her bendy arms in a pub garden on request, but I will!

Then when I am on my deathbed (let's hope it's a bed, I want to die in comfort) and I close my eyes and know my brief time of being alive on this planet is over, I will have a little greatest-hits-of-my-life video playing in my head. Frank Sinatra will sing and I will see black-and-white images of myself. Laughing and waggling my fingers whilst people stand around with their pints laughing too.

Hernia Addendum

Once again, I found myself in the sauna with a number of people, one of whom had been one of the umbilical hernia men.

Had been you say?

Yes, *had* been. His hernia had been replaced with a very neat scar just above his belly button.

I felt glad he hadn't lost his belly button during the surgery.

That universal sign of having had a mother, of not coming from nowhere.

He seemed quite jolly.

That evening in the sauna, someone started a singsong and everyone joined in with rock hits of the 80's.

Lots of people knew many of the words to "Kayleigh" by Marillion, more so than you'd think.

The song ended and the man in the shower (just outside the sauna) tried to start up the singing again with, "*Young girl get out of my mind, my love for you is way out of line.*"

But it was pointed out it was a bit of a paedophile song.

He took it on the chin, finished his shower and left.

I hope he didn't go home and berate himself.

It occurred to me that that there was now only one umbilical hernia man at large. That I know of, of course there would be others. But would I be lucky enough to meet them and view their protrusions on a regular basis? Not unless I become a doctor. I googled "what qualifications do you need to become a doctor?", not for the first time in my life. A list of qualifications came up that I don't think I could complete in my lifetime.

I googled "can I do some sort of conversion course from my Drama Degree to becoming a doctor?". It seems this is also frowned upon; being able to impersonate a doctor is not the same as *being* a doctor it seems... I can however become a "quack doctor". This is a type of doctor that "functions as a doctor but without the qualifications or skills".

So, do you have any protrusions around your belly button?

Would you like me to inspect it for you?

I can tell you now, I might conclude that you need surgery, in which case I will refer you to your GP who will probably know more than me about the ins and outs of it and whatnot. I'll come with you, if you like? Let me just get changed into something more revealing.

Acknowledgments

Thank you to Stephanie Bretherton at Breakthrough Books for letting us publish this weird little book. Thank you to Simon Kane and Dave Williams for reading a draft of it and not having us arrested. Thanks to Jamie and Ivy and Patrick and all the Breakthrough Books gang. You're all superstars. And thanks to all the lovely sauna gang.

If you've bought this and you've read all the way to this bit, are you OK? You look like you have a temperature. How is your belly button? Has it suddenly started protruding? Do you want me to take a look?

www.ingramcontent.com/pod-product-compliance
Lightning Source LLC
Chambersburg PA
CBHW072305130726
47910CB00012B/2438